THE SURROGATE'S UNEXPECTED MIRACLE

BY
ALISON ROBERTS

MILLS
BOON

Published in Great Britain 2017
By Mills & Boon, an imprint of HarperCollins*Publishers*
1 London Bridge Street, London, SE1 9GF

© 2017 Alison Roberts

ISBN: 978-0-263-06935-8

Our policy is to use papers that are natural, renewable and recyclable
products and made from wood grown in sustainable forests. The logging
and manufacturing processes conform to the legal environmental
regulations of the country of origin.

Printed and bound in Great Britain
by CPI Antony Rowe, Chippenham, Wiltshire

Alison Roberts is a New Zealander, currently lucky enough to be living in the south of France. She is also lucky enough to write for the Mills & Boon Medical Romance line. A primary school teacher in a former life, she is also a qualified paramedic. She loves to travel and dance, drink champagne and spend time with her daughter and her friends.

Visit the Author Profile page
at millsandboon.co.uk for more titles.

For Ellie,
with thanks for letting me borrow your name. xx

Praise for
Alison Roberts

'…the author gave me wonderful enjoyable moments of conflict and truth-revealing moments of joy and sorrow… I highly recommend this book for all lovers of romance with medical drama as a backdrop and second-chance love.'
—*Contemporary Romance Reviews* on
NYC Angels: An Explosive Reunion

'This is a deeply emotional book, dealing with difficult life and death issues and situations in the medical community. But it is also a powerful story of love, forgiveness and learning to be intimate… There's a lot packed into this novella. I'm impressed.'
—*Goodreads* on
200 Harley Street: The Proud Italian

CHAPTER ONE

How could so many things have gone so terribly, terribly wrong?

Ellie Thomas could feel the shape of the phone she was holding against her ear. The edges felt sharper as her grip tightened. They were tangible and real.

What she was hearing couldn't possibly be real.

Could it...?

'Ava—are you still there?'

A moment's silence and then she heard her friend's voice again. Her best friend since...since as long as she could remember. A bond that had lasted throughout childhood. Through the trauma of Ava's surgery and chemotherapy as a teenager. With happy memories like being Ava's bridesmaid two years ago and the darker memories of her best mate's despair at not being able to become a mother—a side effect of the treatment that had saved her life.

A friendship that had seemed unbreakable. Until two weeks ago...

'Yeah... I'm still here.' A stifled sob could be heard. 'And... I'm sorry. I'm so sorry, Ellie.'

Sorry? Did that somehow make this okay?

'Where are you?' Ellie could hear the sound of an

announcement of some kind going on in a noisy background. Was Ava at a train station? 'Talk to me, Ave. We can sort this out. I've been trying to call you since the beginning of last week.'

Ever since she had heard that Marco, Ava's gorgeous looking but sometimes volatile husband, had packed a bag and walked out on her.

The day after that awful row... The last time she and Ava and Marco had been in the same room together.

'I was getting frantic,' Ellie added.

Terrified might be a bit closer to the truth.

The silence on the other end of the line was unnerving. Ellie could feel a tight knot of fear that was making it difficult to draw in a new breath. This couldn't be happening. A friendship like this couldn't just evaporate because of something that hadn't even been her fault. Not after all they'd been through together and especially not with what they were going through right now.

'I didn't encourage him, Ava. You *know* that, don't you? I was just as horrified as you were that he tried to kiss me.'

'It wasn't just you.' Ava had stopped crying and there was anger in her low, fierce tone. 'He's been cheating on me the whole time. He admitted it. Said I would never have been enough for a man like him. That our marriage had been a huge mistake because I couldn't accept that.' The tears were obviously flowing again and her next words were totally broken. '...that trying to have a baby was just putting a Band-Aid on a wound that was already fatal.'

Ellie could hear an odd humming and there were bright specks in front of her eyes. Oh, yeah...

Breathe…

'You're not trying to have a baby.' Her words came out in a voice she hardly recognised as her own. 'You *are* having a baby. In about four weeks.'

'But don't you see? I can't do it now. My world's fallen apart, Ellie and I can't hang on to anything. It's not even *my* baby…'

Technically, this was true. Technically, this was Ellie's baby. Ellie and Marco's. The gift that was the one thing that could make life perfect for Ava. It had been such a huge decision, offering to be a surrogate, but Ellie hadn't really hesitated. This was something she could do for the most important person in her life—the only real family she had left.

Fear was morphing into anger, which was a relief because it made it easier to breathe again.

'I'm thirty-six weeks pregnant, Ava. With *your* baby. Yours and Marco's. A baby I would never have dreamed of having otherwise. I'm single, remember? I don't have any family to support me. I don't even have a boyfriend, as you well know. I'm supposed to go back to work in six weeks and if I don't, I won't be able to pay my rent. And you're *sorry*?'

The silence against the background noise was astonishingly loud. Time seemed to be standing still. It could have been seconds but it felt like minutes or even hours. And when it was finally broken, the words Ellie could hear were almost too strangled to understand.

'Got to go…last call…can't miss my plane…'

Fear was strong enough to feel like pain, now.

'*Plane?* Where are you going? Ava…? *Ava?*'

The beeping of a disconnected line said it all but Ellie

couldn't hang up. She lowered the phone and stared at it. Any moment now, the dropped line would be abandoned and she would see the image that was on the screen of her locked phone. The picture of herself and Ava, with their arms around each other, Ava pressing a kiss to her cheek and the smile on Ellie's face making it clear that she was the happiest person in the world.

And there it was...

Ellie dropped the phone on the floor. She wrapped her arms around the huge bump that was her belly now and bent her head to try and deal with the wave of fear and pain that was threatening to wash her over the edge of an unimaginably high cliff.

A pain that was an overwhelming swirl of loss and anger and bewilderment and terror.

It wasn't going to ebb any time soon, either. It filled her chest and made it impossible to breathe again but then it seemed to move to her back as well. And then to her belly, where it gripped harder and harder...

Ellie could feel the muscles under her hands tightening with the strength of a vice. This wasn't just emotional—it was becoming very, very physical.

She was an emergency department nurse, for heaven's sake. She knew what this was but it took another five minutes and the start of another contraction to admit it. When she saw the blood trickling down her leg fast enough to be pooling on the worn linoleum of her floor, she realised just how much trouble she might be in.

Gripping the armrest of her chair, she managed to lower herself onto her knees on the floor and reach for her phone. The call was answered instantly.

'Ambulance... What is your location...?'

* * *

Lucas Gilmore was getting used to pushing through the overgrown shrubs on the front path. He'd find time to trim them soon but there had been more important things to do. Like making the house habitable.

The man walking behind him stopped beside the front steps and brushed pollen and spider webs off the dark trousers of his dress suit. The smile was a little forced but an aspiring leader in local real estate like Mike knew how to disguise distaste.

His smile faded, however, as he turned his head to look at the rambling garden and the exterior of the huge, old wooden villa with its rusting, corrugated iron roof.

'Bit run down, isn't it, Dr Gilmore?'

'Yes. My mother's been in a rest home for several years and the house has been rented out. The agency clearly wasn't doing the job they led me to believe they were doing. The last tenants left nearly a year ago and no maintenance was done, unfortunately. And the inside of the place looked like a bunch of possums had got in through a broken window and had a party.'

'Hmm. You would have done better to use our firm. We're into rentals now.' Mike climbed the steps onto the veranda and a board creaked ominously beneath his feet. 'Hope the inside of the place is in better shape as far as maintenance goes or it's going to be a bit hard to get a good price.'

The smile reappeared. It was almost a grin. 'Having said that, Auckland prices are going completely crazy and it's the land that's going to sell this place. You've got access to an almost private beach and acres of native forest. This is an amazing property. Ripe for re-development.'

Lucas could feel a scowl emerging. Redevelopment was a dirty word for him right now. The house was important. Okay, it might be run down but it was a glorious example of an early nineteenth century New Zealand villa—with return verandas and even a turret, for heaven's sake.

'I'm working on fixing the house. I got commercial cleaners in as soon as I arrived back in the country three weeks ago. The garden's next on the list but I've been a bit busy.'

'Did you say you're working at North Shore General hospital?'

'Yes.' Lucas pushed open a front door in need of a new paint job. 'I took a locum position for three months. I figured that would give me plenty of time to sort things out here.'

And to decide where he wanted to go next to take his career as an emergency specialist to even greater heights.

'And you're sure you want to sell?'

Lucas covered his silence by ushering Mike into the house and walking down the wide hallway with its polished wooden floorboards towards the kitchen at the back. Beams of light made mottled red and green coloured shadows on the wall, thanks to the stained glass window over the door behind him.

Did he want to sell the only house that had ever been a home for him?

No. Of course he didn't. This had been the first place he'd felt wanted. When he was a troubled young teen on the verge of being too old to find another foster home, the Gilmores had taken him in.

And loved him.

It didn't make any difference that he'd kicked off to accelerate the abandonment process before he could get to like the place. And man, there'd been so much to like. The beach with its tempting surf, the secret silence of the beech forest. The generous home-cooked meals. Even having to take a country bus to the nearest high school had been different enough to be fun. It would have been the biggest wrench ever when the inevitable happened and he wasn't wanted any longer.

The Gilmores might have been much older than most foster parents but they had been made of tough stuff and they'd seen something no one else had ever seen. They had decided he was worth the effort.

'You might as well stop acting up,' they'd told him. *'Kicking holes in the walls isn't going to change anything. You're not going anywhere, son. We've adopted you and that's that.'*

But, yes. He did want to sell. There was nothing here for him now. There hadn't been, ever since the death of Eric Gilmore had revealed that he'd been covering the signs of his wife's dementia for some time and the heart breaking decision that Dorothy Gilmore needed specialist care had had to be made. He'd found the best home available as close as possible to where he was living and working.

A shame it was in Sydney, Australia, because it meant taking Dorothy away from the area she'd been born and raised in but the alternative was in Auckland and the biggest city in this country had been just as foreign to Dorothy as Sydney and he certainly couldn't have made his twice-weekly visits. And it hadn't been long before she didn't know who *he* was any more so it really didn't matter what city was outside the walls of her haven.

And—after five years of being cared for so well—Dorothy had died, at the grand old age of ninety-five, just six weeks ago.

It hadn't been a surprise to find that he'd inherited this property that had been rural when he'd arrived about twenty years ago but was now within easy commuting distance of what was touted as one of the most desirable cities in the world to live in. What had been a surprise was the distant cousin, Brian Gilmore, a man in his late sixties, who'd emerged to contest the will.

'You were only a foster kid,' he'd informed Lucas. 'Aunt Dorothy and Uncle Eric never formally adopted you. You've got no right to inherit anything.'

Brian dabbled in property development. This house and its sprawling garden covered an area of land that had enough space for half a dozen properties. Or a retirement village, perhaps, with this perfect, peaceful location and amazing views of the sea and all the islands in the Gulf.

That would only happen after the house was demolished, of course. And probably more than half the native forest bulldozed.

He'd reached the kitchen. A long room with a slate floor and French doors between big windows that looked out over the garden that Dorothy had loved so much. Down to the huge vegetable garden that had been Eric's pride and joy. Amongst other outdoor jobs, his contribution to family chores had been to help Eric manage that garden.

He'd hated it, at first.

He'd actually set fire to the potting shed one evening

but even that hadn't been enough to persuade his new parents that they'd made a mistake.

The wash of loss was hard enough to make Lucas pause and take in a long, slow breath. Dorothy and Eric might have been old enough to be his grandparents when they'd taken him in but they were the only real parents he'd ever had and he'd come to love them fiercely. They'd been so proud of him when they'd come to watch his graduation from medical school.

We knew you could do it, son. We knew you were special.'

'This is nice...' Mike was looking up at the beamed ceiling and then his gaze ran swiftly over the old cooking range and the arched doorway into the big pantry that had once been a creamery for the original farm. He frowned at the masking tape crisscrossing one of the windows where a pane of glass was badly cracked and he was making rapid notes on a tablet device. 'Good thing you left it fully furnished. It looks like someone's living in it and these antiques look original.'

'Some of them probably are,' Lucas agreed. 'And it certainly is a lovely home. It needs to be sold to a family that will love it.' As the Gilmore family had. 'I'm not selling to anyone who wants to demolish this house.'

Brian's words still stung. Maybe Dorothy and Eric hadn't realised what was involved in a formal adoption process. They'd changed his name before enrolling him at his new school and somehow that had been enough and he'd slipped through the system. He'd been Lucas Gilmore ever since.

He'd been their son.

And he wasn't about to let cousin Brian destroy any part of the miracle that had turned his life around so completely. He had his solicitor working on the legality of the unexpected claim and he was hopeful he could have it overturned in court.

A family of his own was never going to happen—he knew too well the nightmare of things going wrong—and even if he had been planning one, it wouldn't be here—where the ghosts of what had gone so wrong in his own early life were never very far away.

But that was what this house needed.

A family. Laughter echoing through the rooms and love to be celebrated in meals taken at this old, scrubbed pine table.

Hopefully, what was left of the three months he had signed up for at Auckland General would be long enough to see that happen. As if prompted by the thought, he turned his head to where the grandfather clock in the hallway was ticking again. A slow, steady sound that had always been the heartbeat of this old house.

'How 'bout I leave you to have a look around at the rest of the place, Mike? If you pull the front door closed, it'll lock itself. I'm due to start my shift in Emergency in less than an hour and you never know what the traffic's going to be like on the motorway. I'd better get my skates on.'

If she hadn't been so frightened, Ellie would have been mortified, arriving at any emergency department like this, let alone the one she worked in herself!

She was on a narrow ambulance stretcher. On her knees, with her head on her hands and her bottom up in the air.

Knowing she was bleeding had been enough to scare

Lower the head of the bed, too. And get some oxygen on the mother.'

The *mother*? Ellie squeezed her eyes tightly shut. She wasn't supposed to be about to become the mother. This was a nightmare. Maybe she'd wake up in a minute to find Ava and Marco standing there. Smiling. Excited to be about to meet their new baby...

This was a slightly more dignified position, at least, but she still had a restricted visual field. She could see the length of the body in dark green scrubs beside her, but it wasn't until he crouched that she could see the face that belonged to that new voice. Tanned skin. Kind of wild brown hair with blond streaks. Hazel eyes. He looked like he'd just come out of some surf, on a hot summer's day, with a board casually slung under one arm.

'Hi, Ellie. I'm Luke Gilmore, one of the doctors here. I'm just going to have a look and see what's going on, okay?'

As another contraction gathered force, Ellie could only nod.

Luke Gilmore? He had to be new here. A locum? She'd stopped work three weeks ago to rest and pre-pare for the birth so she hadn't met him. She hadn't even heard his name.

Or had she? It did seem vaguely familiar...

With the contraction reaching its peak, the thought was obliterated by pain. She pushed her fist into her mouth but couldn't stifle a cry.

For a long moment, nothing existed except the pain but then she became aware of the voices around her.

'What was the time interval for that last contraction?'

'Two minutes.'

'Estimated blood loss?'

'Five hundred mils on scene.' The paramedics were still there. 'We put in a wide bore IV and she's had a litre of saline so far.'

'She's still bleeding. Let's get another litre going.'

That was this Dr Gilmore's voice. Did he know what he was doing? He certainly sounded confident enough. Ellie could feel that her lower body was bare now. Maybe it was a good thing that she didn't know this person but there were plenty of people she did know seeing a lot more of her than they ever had before. Not that she cared. Nothing mattered right now other than to get through this safely. There was a baby's life at stake. Maybe even her own, if she was still losing so much blood.

She could feel a hand inside her.

'Ah...' The sound was hard to interpret. Satisfaction...or concern? 'Ellie? You're going to feel me pushing. I need to take the pressure off the cord.'

He still sounded calm, this Luke. And she could feel him pushing hard against the baby's head.

'Any risk factors in the pregnancy?'

'Not that we know of.' The paramedic sounded embarrassed. It was a question they should have asked.

'Low lying placenta,' Ellie said, but her voice was muffled behind the oxygen mask.

'Sorry, what was that?' Luke was still pushing against her baby's head to ensure it was clear of the cord but he leaned sideways so that she could see his face as she turned her head. In the bustle of people and activity around her, there was something very calming in the steady gaze of those hazel eyes that were visible again.

'I've had a low-lying placenta. Only marginal but

I was due for another scan this week and possible admission for observation and a C section if indicated.'

She saw the flicker of surprise in his eyes at her clinical information.

'Ellie's a nurse,' someone behind him said. Sue had come into the resus area. 'She's one of our best ED nurses, in fact.'

Luke's face disappeared from her line of sight. 'Where's our Obs consult?'

'Here.' A female voice who sounded rather nervous.

'This is Anne Duffy,' Sue said. 'O&G registrar.'

Maybe Luke had picked up on the nervousness. 'Have you got a theatre available? We've got a cord prolapse here. She's fully dilated but still in stage one. We're looking at either an emergency C section or an operative delivery.'

'No.' Anne sounded young as well as nervous. 'We're in the middle of a C section for triplets. It's got most of our staff tied up for a while but it shouldn't be too long until one of the consultants is available. Is the baby distressed?'

Maybe it was her imagination but Ellie thought she heard Luke sigh. 'Have we got that foetal monitor hooked up yet?'

'Yes. Baby's heart-rate is one-thirty. No, hang on... one-ten... It's dropping...'

Ellie could feel her own heart-rate increasing. This was suddenly getting very serious. If the baby's heart-rate was dropping, it meant that the head was finally putting too much pressure on the cord despite the interventions. The clock was ticking now...

And something else was changing.

'I need to push,' she said.

'Don't push.' The registrar definitely sounded nervous now. Terrified, even? 'Take deep breaths. Try and go limp. Relax your pelvic floor.'

If Ellie had had any spare breath right then, it might have come out as an incredulous huff. Just how much experience had this junior doctor had? She fought the urge to push, her face scrunched as tightly as possible against the pain.

'Heart-rate's down to eighty,' someone said.

'Not too long isn't good enough.' There was a different note in Luke's voice now. He had made a decision and was taking control. 'Lay out the forceps kit, please. Can someone put out an urgent page and get a paediatrician down here, stat? Anne—take over here. Two fingers on the baby's head and upward pressure, okay?'

'Got it.'

'Have you done a forceps delivery?'

'I've assisted with one.'

'Ellie? Can you hear me?'

'Y-yes.' Her voice came out sounding oddly croaky. Frightened...

Luke was crouched right beside her now, his face only a few inches from her own.

'We need to get your baby out as soon as possible. You're fully dilated and with the help of forceps we can do it. I've done a long stint in obstetrics and have experience in assisted delivery. Are you happy for me to go ahead?'

There was nothing about this that Ellie was happy about. But there was something in those eyes that gave her something to cling to.

Confidence. Hope...

She nodded, giving her consent.

'We can give you some Entonox but there's no time for any other pain relief to kick in. It's going to be a bit rough. I'm sorry…'

He was sorry. He looked as though he would take that impending pain himself rather than inflict it on her. Ellie closed her eyes to hold back tears but she nodded again. 'It's okay…'

She could feel the tension in the room around her. Hear the clatter of instrument kits being unrolled onto a stainless steel trolley. She felt her body being moved so that she was lying on her back, sterile drapes being folded around her and listened to the instructions Luke was issuing as her legs were lifted and supported.

And he talked to her all through it, too.

'I'm giving you a bit of local for the episiotomy. You'll feel it sting for a moment.'

It stung a lot but Ellie knew it was only the start. She sucked on the mouthpiece giving her the inhaled pain relief.

'I'm inserting the first blade, now. And the second. And I'm locking them. When the next contraction starts, I'm going to need you to push—as hard as you can, sweetheart.'

Sweetheart?

The word cut through the fear and pain. It was just a word that should have evaporated into the ether the moment it had been spoken but it didn't. It echoed in her head and sent ripples through her body. It was something warm and caring and lovely in the middle of something horrific. And when the instruction to push came moments after the next contraction started she pushed with every ounce of strength she could summon.

And maybe she found more strength than she knew

she had because, in the wake of being abandoned by the person she cared about most, he'd called her sweetheart...

It only took two contractions, a minute apart, with her pushing as if her life depended on it and Luke pulling with the baby's head cradled between the blades of the forceps and she could feel the baby coming into the world.

'It's a boy, Ellie,' someone said.

She knew that. Marco and Ava had known that, too. They'd already picked out a name. Carlos.

Her train of thought vanished as she became aware of the silence in the room. There was no baby crying. And nobody else was saying anything, either. The silence was shocked. And shocking. Ellie jerked her head up to see a tiny, limp body that someone was rubbing briskly with a towel.

A woman she didn't know—the nervous young registrar, perhaps—saw her looking.

'It's okay, Ellie. We're doing everything we can for your baby.'

Tears that had been building for too long exploded from Ellie as she let her head drop back down.

'But he's *not* my baby,' she sobbed. 'And now *nobody* wants him...'

CHAPTER TWO

WHAT?

Surely he hadn't heard correctly?

For a split second, Lucas froze, completely distracted from what he was about to do.

Nobody wanted this baby?

One of the department's senior nurses, Sue, was right beside him.

'This was a surrogate pregnancy,' she told him quietly. 'But I have no idea what's gone wrong.'

Lucas couldn't give a damn about what might have gone wrong. There was a knot in his chest that felt like anger.

He knew what it was like to be an unwanted child. To face a world where you were not worth enough for anybody to want you.

No more than a blink of time had passed but Lucas snapped back to reality.

'Give him to me,' he snapped.

Picking up the limp bundle, he carried it to the trolley that had been hastily prepared with neonatal resuscitation gear. He gently laid the tiny body onto the sterile drapes. The miniature mask seemed to cover half the face as he delivered puffs of oxygen. He put his hands around a chest that felt alarmingly fragile, position-ing both his thumbs on the sternum. Gentle but rapid compressions. Sue had followed him and picked up the mask. One puff, three compressions. One puff, three compressions.

You can do it... Come on... Fight...it's worth it, I promise...

Only Luke could hear the words in his head. Or were they coming from his heart?

Someone's going to love you...

There weren't any words that came with his next thought—it was just a flash of sensation that came from nowhere.

I love you...

He shook off the bizarre notion. Getting emotionally involved in this unexpected case wasn't going to help anyone. He needed to think ahead. Professionally. Intu-bation as the next step... IV access through the umbili-cal cord...chasing up that specialist paediatric consult...

And then the miracle happened. He felt the tiny body move between his hands. He paused the compressions and felt the push of that little ribcage against the pads of his thumbs as the baby took its own first breath.

And then another. That tiny face scrunched itself into an angry expression and the third breath was enough to provide the power for a warbling sound. The next effort was much more convincing.

This little guy was a fighter, after all.

And then Luke heard another cry from a very unex-pected direction. From behind him.

From this new mother who didn't want this baby.

He could feel his face tightening as he turned. His heart hardening.

And then he saw her face.

Propped up on her elbows, Ellie must have been watching this whole resuscitation effort and she had definitely heard those first sounds of a new life awakening.

Her hair was a tangle of blonde knots around a face that was pale enough to suggest she had lost a concerning amount of blood. And those eyes...

Huge, dark blue pools that were telling him something very different than the last words he had heard her speaking—that this wasn't her baby and that nobody wanted him.

These were the eyes of a desperate woman. A mother...

'Please,' she whispered... 'Please can I hold my baby?'

It had been that sound that had done it.

The cry from that tiny human that had been nestled within her body for so many months had taken the world as Ellie knew it and tipped it upside down. It had entered her ears but gone straight to her heart and captured it in the fiercest imaginable grip.

For a long, long moment, caught in what felt like a very disapproving stare from the doctor who'd just delivered her son, she thought that she was facing an impenetrable barrier. Someone who had no intention of letting her close to that tiny being she could just catch a glimpse of behind the solid figure of this new doctor.

But Sue was picking the baby up now.

'Apgar score is ten at five minutes,' she said, unable to keep a grin off her face. She was wrapping the baby in soft towels. 'He's looking great. I think we could let

Mum have a bit of skin contact, until our paediatrician arrives, don't you think?'

Luke's response was a huff of sound that seemed indecisive but the anticipation of holding her baby against her own skin was so overwhelming that Ellie's breath escaped in something that sounded like a sob as she lay back and held her arms out.

'The placenta's delivered.' The young registrar was sounding a lot more confident now. 'Seems intact and the bleeding's almost stopped. Let's prop you up a bit so you can hold your baby.'

Ellie had barely registered the last contractions as she watched the frantic efforts to save her son. Everything was all right now, though. She wasn't about to bleed to death and the baby's perfect Apgar score meant that he had come through this crisis with flying colours. With pillows being layered behind her, she was more than ready to accept the precious bundle that Sue was bringing towards her.

But why was this new doctor in her department still staring at her as if she was asking for something she really didn't deserve?

He'd called her sweetheart only minutes ago.

Before helping her deliver her baby. Before he'd saved her life. Before he'd even properly begun to start saving the life of that baby.

And then something filtered into her brain. An echo of her own voice...

'But he's not my baby... And now nobody wants him...'

Oh, God...had she really said that?

No wonder he thought she was crazy. Or some kind of monster.

But Sue was beside her now and everybody else in this room and whatever tasks they were attending to ceased to exist as far as Ellie was concerned. Sue was unwrapping the tiny body of her baby, and another nurse was helping to remove the oversized tee shirt Ellie had been wearing. And her bra.

And there he was. In her arms and snuggled against her bare chest, while Sue arranged some soft, fluffy blankets around them both for warmth and as much privacy as was possible, given the surroundings.

Ellie couldn't even lift her head to smile her thanks. Her baby's eyes were open and he was staring up at her and nothing could have induced her to break that astonishing eye contact.

'Hullo, you...' she whispered. 'I'm Mummy.'

The wash of emotion was like nothing Ellie had ever experienced. Something was changing in her body at a cellular level and she would never be the same person she'd been only minutes ago.

Who knew that love could be *this* powerful? So huge...and every bit of it was for this tiny little human.

Had she really believed she could have given him to someone else?

This baby was a part of herself and she would fight to the death if necessary to protect him.

It was the baby who finally broke that intense eye contact. His head bobbed against the arm it was cradled by and his tiny mouth opened and closed against the skin of Ellie's breast. Instinctively, she adjusted her position, which brought her nipple within range of the baby's mouth. And then she watched, in astonishment, as the baby found what it was seeking and latched on to her nipple as though he'd done it many times before.

Ellie's jaw dropped. 'He did that all by himself.'

'He's a genius.' Sue smiled. 'Oh…where's my phone? We've got to get a photo of this.'

But Ellie had closed her eyes by the time Sue had fished her phone from the pocket of her scrub pants and she could feel a tear escape and roll down the side of her nose. And then another.

This feeling—the silky new born skin against her own, the shape of those tiny limbs within her arms and, most of all, the tug of that tiny mouth against her breast—was too much.

It felt like pure joy…

Luke had rather a lot of paperwork to do to document this emergency delivery that had happened on his watch. Someone had given him the forms on a clipboard and he had a pen in his hand but he hadn't written a word, yet.

He kept looking sideways. From where he was standing, beside the trolley they'd used to resuscitate this baby, he could see the back of the baby's head nestled in the crook of Ellie's arms.

And he could see Ellie's face.

She had no idea he was watching her. Luke doubted that she was aware of anything other than the baby she was holding.

They seemed to be staring at each other. Locked in a conversation that was so utterly private that Luke felt uncomfortable observing it.

So he looked away.

Eleanor Thomas, someone had filled in under the personal details on the form. Thirty-two years old. Thirty-six weeks pregnant.

He had to look back. It was none of his business that there was something weird going on. A surrogate pregnancy?

Who for?

Why?

And what had gone so wrong that she'd claimed that nobody wanted this child now?

It certainly didn't look as if nobody wanted him.

Ellie looked, for all the world, as if she was in the middle of a personal miracle. Mesmerised by the face of her child. As though this baby was being bathed in as much love as it was possible for any person to bestow.

It was weird, all right. And disturbing on a level that Luke hadn't expected. Maybe it was because this was happening so soon after he'd been standing in the home it had taken so many years for him to find.

Had his own mother looked at him like that in the minutes after he'd been born?

No. He'd always known the answer to that.

This time it was easier to look away. To try and focus on the paperwork.

Surely no mother could ever look at her child like that and then simply hand him to strangers when life got tough and never even try to see him again? Had it even occurred to his mother that the scars of being abandoned and finding himself unwanted would be there for the rest of his life?

The paediatrician arrived and Luke gave him a verbal handover. He still had the notes to write up on the baby's early resuscitation as well.

The new arrival looked at Ellie, who was now breast-feeding the infant, and he was smiling.

'I think we can get them up to the ward before we examine baby properly. He's looking pretty happy.'

Anne, the O&G registrar, had joined them. She was nodding. 'I'll leave the repair of the episiotomy until then, too. I'll see what rooms we have available and order a transfer.'

Within minutes, the transfer had been arranged. The bed, with the baby still cradled in Ellie's arms, was being wheeled out of the resuscitation room and staff members were already busy cleaning up. Luke heard the metallic clang as the forceps and other instruments he had used were dropped into a container to be sent for sterilisation. Blood stained towels and drapes were going into the contaminated linen bag and a cleaner began mopping the floor. A new bed was outside, waiting to take centre stage in a room that would have no evidence of the life and death drama that had just occurred.

Another one would probably take its place very soon but this one was over. Any odd personal connection he might have felt needed to be dismissed. He had done his job and whatever lay ahead for Ellie and her baby was none of his business.

Well, it wasn't quite over yet. With a sigh, Luke picked up the clipboard. He could finish this paperwork in the office and, if he was lucky, it would be done before he was needed elsewhere. He didn't want to be here, tying up loose ends like this, when his shift finished late in the evening.

A visitor was the last thing Ellie was expecting at this time of night.

It was after ten p.m. and she was propped up on her

pillows, in the soft glow of the night light in her private room, and she was doing nothing more than being in the moment. Listening to the soft snuffles and squeaks coming from the tiny bundle in the plastic bassinet that was within touching distance of her bed. Trying to absorb this momentous change in her life.

She thought the soft tap on her door would be one of the nursing staff, coming to check that everything was okay and that she was ready to try and get some sleep. When Luke Gilmore stepped into her room, she was too astonished to even say hullo.

'Is this a bad time? They told me on the desk that you'd just finished a feed and would probably still be awake.'

Ellie was still staring at him. It was obvious she was still awake so there didn't seem to be anything that needed to be said. She could feel a puzzled frown creasing her brow.

Why was he here? Most emergency department doctors—especially locums—didn't have the time or the interest in following up their cases. They treated them and moved them on, job done. There were always more to take their places.

But it was nice that he wanted to check up on them. Ellie's lips curved into a smile, which was taken as an invitation to come into the room, but then the smile wobbled.

Had he come to have a go at her for what had been said in a moment of both physical and emotional agony? When this whole, sorry story of her attempt to be a surrogate mother had looked as if it was about to end in disaster?

He didn't look as if he was angry about anything.

Closing the door softly behind him, Luke stepped towards her bed, stopping to gaze down at the sleeping, snuffling baby.

Ellie found herself gazing at *him*. There was something about those rather craggy features and that shaggy hair that seemed very familiar. Had he worked in the same hospital as her in the past, maybe? Way back, when she was newly qualified and too focused on doing her job well to take much notice of staff members in other departments?

'I hear he passed his paediatric check with flying colours.'

'Mmm.' Ellie found both her voice and another smile. 'He's perfect. A good weight, too, even though he was four weeks early. He's almost seven pounds.'

She was still trawling through dim memory banks.

Luke Gilmore...doctor...

Or not yet a doctor?

'Oh, my God...' Ellie breathed. 'You're *Lucas* Gilmore, aren't you?'

Startled eyes met her own. 'Ah...yes. But I haven't been called Lucas in about fifteen years. By anyone other than my parents, that is...'

'You went to Kauri Valley District High School?'

His face had gone very still. He didn't say anything but he was frowning—as though he was searching his own memory banks as he stared at her face.

'I went there, too. You won't remember me—I was a couple of years behind you. But we shared the school bus every day. You lived on the coast, didn't you? Near Moana Beach?'

Uninvited, Luke sank to balance his hip on the end of Ellie's bed, one arm over the base board, his fingers touching the clip of the board that held her observations chart.

'No way... Wait... I *do* remember you. You always sat up the front. You had really long plaits.'

The thought that he'd noticed her at all on a crowded bus made Ellie feel suddenly shy. She would have died if she'd known it at the time. Lucas Gilmore—Kauri Valley high school's bad boy—aware of *her* existence? It would have been scary. And...thrilling?

'You always sat right at the back,' she heard herself saying. 'With all the cool kids.'

'The ones who got into trouble, you mean?'

There was something intense in his glance now. Did he want to know how much Ellie knew about the kind of trouble he'd been in as a kid?

Okay, she knew quite a lot. Ellie could almost hear an echo of her mother's voice.

'Stay away from that Gilmore boy. He's bad news. Nothing but trouble...'

She wasn't about to say anything now, though. He'd clearly turned his life around. He was a doctor, for heaven's sake. A doctor who'd just saved the lives of both herself and her baby.

There was a flash of something like relief on Luke's features as she shrugged his comment away. She could sense the tension ebbing away from his body. Or maybe she could feel it, as the mattress dipped with his settling weight.

'You were always with another girl who always wore hats.'

Ellie nodded. 'Ava. My best friend. Her hair was never the same after all the chemo she had and it took her a long time to get used to it.'

'Chemo? What for?'

'Leukaemia.'

'Did she survive?'

'Oh, yeah… And her hair came back even better than ever. Turned out that she'd never be able to have kids, though.'

The sudden stillness in Luke's face told her that he'd put two and two together with remarkable speed. Almost as though he was reading her mind.

'That's who you were being a surrogate for?'

Ellie nodded. She had to bite her lip to push back the wash of loss. Ava had been such a big part of her life for ever and now she had gone and it was going to leave a gaping hole.

'Wow…' She listened to the deep breath that Luke took and then let out in a long sigh as he pushed his fingers through that mop of sun-streaked hair. The front locks immediately flopped down onto his forehead again. 'That's an incredible thing to do for a friend. *Huge…*'

There was a long silence. It had to be obvious that she was struggling to keep herself together right now. Most strangers would have probably realised they were intruding in something very personal and made some kind of apology and then an excuse to let her have some time to herself or an offer to find someone she wanted to talk to. But Luke just sat there quietly. Absorbing her struggle. Offering his company and what felt like… empathy?

'It's all gone so terribly wrong,' she found herself whispering into the silence. 'Her husband walked out on her a couple of weeks ago. The marriage is over. And now Ava's gone, too. Just gone…' She had to stop and take a very shaky breath. 'And I can't really blame her. She's devastated and, as she told me, it's not really *her* baby. It was *my* egg. And now...now it's *my* baby and... and I have no idea what I'm going to do...'

Luke's frown had deepened but he was still listening. Nodding very slowly. 'And the father?'

'Marco? I don't think he's coming back. Apparently he said he'd never really wanted a baby in the first place.' Ellie's voice was stronger now. She was on much more solid ground. 'And I don't want him to.'

An eyebrow quirked under that shaggy fringe but Ellie saw the subtle lift of the corners of Luke's mouth. He liked what he was hearing, she realised, and that made her want to say a whole lot more.

'I thought I could do it, you know? Donate an egg and carry a baby for someone else. I thought I could hand him over the minute he was born and then just be... I don't know...a kind of auntie, I guess. We'd planned to tell him eventually. When he was old enough to understand.'

'But...?'

'It was when I heard him cry...' Again, Ellie had to stop talking to try and deal with the flood of emotion but, this time, it wasn't anything to do with loss or grief. This was joy, pure and simple. 'That was when I knew that this was *my* baby. That I could never give him away. That he's...he's the most important thing in my life now...'

Ellie had to scrub away an errant tear but it didn't matter. Luke looked as though he was blinking back some extra moisture in his own eyes. And his voice sounded a bit rusty when he spoke again.

'Have you given him a name?'

Ellie sniffed inelegantly and then smiled. 'I had the best dad in the world. He was a forestry worker and got killed in an industrial accident when I was only six but I've never forgotten how much he loved me. How much I loved him. His name was James but everyone called him Jamie.' She had to use the fingers of both hands to wipe her cheeks this time. 'So that's what I'm going to call him. Jamie.'

As if he'd heard his name, the baby stirred and started to cry. Ellie turned and leaned towards the bassinet but then froze, unable to stop her gasp of pain. It wasn't just the stitches in a very tender place. Her whole body felt bruised and battered right now.

'Let me...'

Luke got to his feet in a smooth movement that was both relaxed and confident. He picked up the swaddled bundle of baby but he didn't immediately hand him to Ellie. He stood there, holding the baby in his arms, patting him gently as he smiled down at the tiny face.

'Hi, Jamie,' he said softly. 'Welcome to the world...'

Jamie hiccupped and then stopped crying. Luke stopped patting and started rubbing the baby's back, his hand looking huge against the small bundle.

'You made a bit of a dramatic entrance,' Luke continued quietly, still smiling. 'You had us a bit worried there for a while, mate.'

Ellie was lying back on her pillows as the pain subsided. There was something about watching this big man holding her tiny baby that was doing funny things to her heart and making her want to cry all over again.

Her hormones were all over the place right now, weren't they?

And then she felt her cheeks flush. 'I haven't even

said thank you,' she said. 'You saved Jamie's life...probably mine, too.'

It seemed as if Jamie had gone back to sleep but Luke didn't put him back into the bassinet. He perched on the bed again, holding the bundle as if it was the most natural thing in the world to do.

'It was my pleasure,' he said. 'The best job I've had since I came back.'

So had they been just a 'job' to him? Just another case and one that would be remembered for snatching success from imminent disaster? Oddly, the disappointment felt crushing.

'Back?' Ellie was relieved to achieve a casual tone.

'I've been working in Australia pretty much since I graduated from medical school. I've taken a three month locum here because I needed some time to sort my parents' estate. And I was ready for a change so it's a good time to take a break and reassess my future.'

So he was a locum. And he was only here for three months.

'I've heard about a couple of great positions already,' he continued. 'I'm tossing up whether I want to apply for the one in London or Boston right now. Both of them are in major trauma centres that deal with things you'd be lucky to ever see in Auckland.'

The disappointment was still there, ready to roll in on another wave. How weird was that? Was it because he represented a link to the past? They'd been to the same school. They would know a lot of the same people in the area Ellie had grown up in. She'd already lost so many links to that happy part of her early life and it had seemed as if the last one had gone with Ava's disappearance.

She swallowed hard. 'Yeah... I guess that's exactly what I have to do now. Reassess my future.'

A whimper from the baby prompted Luke to move. This time he transferred the bundle into Ellie's arms. And then he caught her gaze. He didn't have to say anything.

She was holding her future.

'Are you going to manage?' he asked quietly. 'Have you got family and friends to support you?'

'No family,' Ellie said. 'But I've got some good friends. You've met Sue, in ED? Well, she's organising an emergency baby shower. I don't have anything. Not even a nappy...'

She had to look away from that steady gaze. She didn't want him to know how terrifying it was. In a day or two, she had to take this brand new little person back to a totally inappropriate inner city apartment where there was barely enough room for herself, let alone a baby and all the gear she was going to need, like a cot and a pram and stacks of nappies.

She didn't even know how she was going to pay the rent on that apartment...

Luke was pulling a pen from the top pocket of his scrubs. He fished out a small notebook and ripped out a page.

'This is my phone number,' he told her. 'If you ever need help, ring me.'

Ellie's eyes widened.

Luke grinned. 'No, I don't usually do this for my patients. But you're special. You're an old bus buddy so we go way back, even if my memory's a bit hazy.'

Ellie pressed her lips together. Her memory was getting less hazy by the minute. She had noticed Luke every time he'd sauntered down the bus aisle past her seat. The bad boy who'd been expelled from every school he'd been to until he got to Kauri Valley. The angry kid who'd somehow morphed into the coolest one. The one that every girl had been desperate to be with...

He put the scrap of paper on the top of her locker.

'Want me to get someone for you? Do you need help with Jamie? Or some pain relief or anything?'

'I think I'm ready to sleep,' Ellie told him. 'Jamie seems to be settled again. Could you put him back in the bassinet for me, please?'

She watched as he carefully positioned the baby on his side and then tucked the sheet securely around him. There was nothing more he needed to do but he paused for a long moment—that big, artistic looking hand cupping the baby's head so gently that the spikes of dark hair barely moved. Ellie could feel that touch herself and it felt as if it were cupping her heart.

He was quite something now, this grown up bad boy.

'Sweet dreams, little guy,' Luke murmured.

And then, with a smile, he was gone, letting himself out of Ellie's room as quietly as he'd come in. He left the door slightly ajar and she could hear the muted sounds of a maternity ward on night shift. The distant cry of another baby. Soft-soled shoes going past in the corridor.

Her baby was asleep and she needed to rest herself. It was the only opportunity she was going to get to heal and gather her strength for what lay ahead.

Adjusting her body to find a more comfortable position, Ellie could see the top of her locker where that scrap of paper lay beside her water glass.

He'd said they were 'bus buddies', she remembered.

He'd said that she was *special*...

He'd given her his phone number to use if she needed help.

Not that she would, but having it there somehow made her immediate future look a little less terrifying.

Ellie drifted into much-needed sleep unaware of the curve of her lips.

She was *special...*

CHAPTER THREE

THE BABY WAS about six weeks old.

A little girl, called Grace, but that didn't stop Luke Gilmore being instantly reminded of Jamie Thomas.

It had been more than two weeks since he'd delivered Ellie's baby in such a dramatic fashion. It felt like a long time since he'd shared what seemed like a surprisingly intimate conversation, late that night in her room.

He would never have recognised Ellie from that time in his past. What he had been prompted to remember was a girl with long blonde braids who had been too timid to interest him. The girl who wore the hats—Ava—used to stare at him but Ellie was also memorable for the way she avoided eye contact.

She hadn't been avoiding it the other night. Quite the opposite. When she had been telling him about the surrogacy arrangement that had gone so wrong and particularly when she'd explained how hearing the baby's first cry had changed her for ever, she'd held his gaze with an intensity that had made him feel as if he was glimpsing a part of her soul.

A courageous soul, he had realised. And a generous one.

She'd been prepared to do something for a friend

that went way beyond the normal boundaries of friendship. And she hadn't been planning to raise a child on her own but was facing what could be a difficult future with such determination—and such obvious love for the baby she had now claimed as purely her own.

He had to admire that.

To admire Ellie.

And, man…as he'd kept going back to that time together in his head—more often than he was comfortable with, to be honest—he realised that Ellie had matured into a very attractive young woman. Her hair was more honey than white blonde now and, thanks to her avoidance of eye contact, he'd never noticed how astonishingly blue her eyes were. There was a softness about her features, too, that he could imagine being the result of a timid, sensitive teenager gaining confidence with time.

This baby who had just come into the emergency department of North Shore General was crying miserably. So was the mother who was holding her as the nurse, Sue, helped to settle her on the bed. The young father was hovering on the other side of the bed, looking stressed and helpless.

'We thought it was just a cold,' he told Luke. 'But now she's got this horrible cough and it sounds like she can't breathe…'

'Has anyone else in the family been unwell?' Luke was looking carefully at the baby as Sue undressed her. The baby looked dehydrated but not feverish and, thankfully, there were no signs of a rash that could be meningococcal.

'I've had a bit of a cough,' the father said. 'Nothing major. Just one of those irritating dry coughs that won't go away. I heard someone call it the "Hundred Day" cough.'

Luke's heart sank as he met Sue's glance as she helped position the baby so that he could put his stethoscope on the tiny chest. For adults or immunised people, the 'Hundred Day' cough was an irritating bug. For babies like this, it could be the life-threatening bacterial infection of whooping cough.

And, sure enough, the baby started coughing. It was too young to have the strength to produce the characteristic 'whooping' sound of gasping for air between the coughing spasms but they were severe enough to be causing a dangerous lack of oxygen and both Luke and Sue watched with deepening concern as the blue tinge to the baby's face advertised a degree of cyanosis that was going to need urgent management.

'See if we've got an oxygen hood in the department,' Luke said to Sue. 'And put out a call for an urgent paediatric consult.'

'I'm going to take a swab,' he told the mother, 'and some blood tests but it looks very likely that she has pertussis—whooping cough. We're going to need to admit her and keep her in isolation.'

'Whooping cough?' The mother looked terrified. 'But that's impossible. I had the booster vaccination that they recommend when you're pregnant. They said that would help keep her safe until she gets her first shot next week.'

'And it does help. You did exactly the right thing.' Luke nodded. 'Did everybody in your extended family get boosters, too?'

'My mother did. I told Gerry that he should get one

but...' The woman glanced up at her husband, who was looking stricken. 'I guess we kind of forgot...'

'Work's been crazy,' he muttered. 'And what with Serena having to give up her job, I've had to take all the overtime I could get.' He turned away, putting his hand over his eyes. 'Oh... God...is this *my* fault?'

'The important thing is looking after little Grace, here.' Luke was pulling supplies from the containers on the bench in this resuscitation area. A tourniquet, the smallest cannula available for IV access, tape and the connecting plug that would enable him to set up a drip. 'We're going to start her on antibiotics without waiting for the test results. And we're going to try and improve her oxygen levels. You must have noticed the way she's going blue with the coughing fits? That means she's not getting enough oxygen and that can be dangerous.'

Another nurse came in with the oxygen hood that Luke had requested.

'We'll get you to put Grace on the bed by herself, now,' Luke said gently. 'This looks scary but it's just a plastic dome that will go over her head on the bed. It's an easier way to provide extra oxygen than taping prongs into her nose.'

It was clearly hard for the mother to hand her baby into the care of others and step back, out of touching range. Her husband put his arms around her as she sobbed.

'Can we stay?' he asked. 'Is that all right?'

'Of course,' Luke said. 'And I'll tell you what we're doing every step of the way. The first thing we need to do is to put a tiny needle into one of Grace's veins. Given how small she is, it might need to go into a vein in her scalp, or her foot, but don't be alarmed. It's just the same as putting one in an adult's arm.'

The new nurse was staying to help Sue hold the baby as Luke began to work on starting treatment that would, hopefully, save this baby from the potentially life-threatening complications from whooping cough that were running through his head right now. Luke had seen babies develop pneumonia and encephalitis from this disease. He'd once looked after a baby in Intensive Care who had needed extracorporeal membrane oxygenation, even, where the blood was removed from the body to do the work of the lungs in the same way a heart-lung bypass machine worked.

The sad thing was that this was a preventable disease but he could understand how the idea of having a booster vaccination had seemed unimportant to the father of this baby.

With the cannula safely secured into a scalp vein, Luke had a moment of distraction with the automatic process of attaching the IV line and setting the drip rate of the fluids.

Had Ellie had a booster vaccination while she was pregnant? How many visitors was little Jamie getting and was he in close enough contact with any of them to be in danger of having something like this passed on? A sideways glance at Sue, who was positioning the plastic dome of the oxygen hood over Grace's head, prompted Luke to make a mental note to talk to her about it. Ellie had told him that Sue was a good friend of hers. She could, at least, pass on the warning that they'd had a serious case here.

The paediatric team arrived and took over the care of Grace and her transfer to their intensive care unit but it wasn't until much later in the evening, after dealing with a man having a heart attack and a motorbike accident victim with a serious leg fracture, that Luke had the time to grab both a coffee in the staffroom and to have a word with Sue, who also happened to be in the room.

'How's Ellie?' The query was casual. 'And Jamie?'

Sue's eyes widened. Was she surprised that he had remembered the name of one patient amongst so many? Or that he knew the name she had given to her baby? He concentrated on stirring his coffee. She would be a lot more than surprised if she knew how often he'd been thinking about them both since then.

'She's amazing.' Sue's expression softened into admiration. 'I can't believe how well she's doing. She wasn't supposed to be keeping this baby so she had nothing, you know? Not even a nappy. And she's living in this tiny apartment that's not much more than a bedsit.'

The movement of Luke's spoon slowed. He could feel relief softening his muscles. If Ellie was doing well maybe he could stop worrying that Jamie wouldn't end up being put up for adoption. Or worse, going into the first of a series of foster homes...

But then he found something else to focus on. Just how tiny was the apartment she was living in? He was rattling around in a huge old house all by himself. How unfair was that?

'She hasn't got any family to help, though, has she?'

'How did you know that? Oh, yeah... I remember now. Ellie said that you'd been to visit while she was in hospital. That you knew each other from way back?'

'We didn't exactly know each other. We used to catch the same school bus, that's all.'

Sue nodded, glancing at her watch. 'I'd better get back. Break's over.'

'You don't know whether Ellie had a pertussis booster while she was pregnant, do you?'

Sue paused. He could see her make the connection with the case they'd both worked on earlier this evening and her nod told him that she knew exactly what he was concerned about. If she was surprised by that ongoing concern, she didn't show it.

'I'll check. You're right. If the bug's in the community at the moment, she needs to know.'

'Anyone else that has close contact with the baby should get a booster, too. Like her boyfriend?'

'Oh, she's safe enough on that score.' Sue was already heading for the door. 'Being single was one of the reasons it was easy for her to make the decision to be a surrogate. And she certainly hasn't had the inclination *or* opportunity to start anything since.'

Luke finally took a mouthful of his rapidly cooling coffee.

'Something up?' One of his registrars came into the staffroom.

'No…why?'

'You're looking worried.'

Luke shook his head. 'All good, mate. And it's nearly home time. What would I have to worry about?'

He abandoned the coffee and went back into the department. What would he have to worry about?

It really wasn't his problem that Ellie might be struggling to cope with limited resources and space.

That she didn't even have a partner to provide more than intermittent assistance...

It was highly unlikely that she would think of calling him if she needed help. As he'd explained to Sue, they hadn't really known each other all those years ago, so why would she?

She probably hadn't even kept his phone number.

It was right there on her fridge door, half hidden by a smiley face magnet.

Luke's phone number.

Ellie spotted it on one of her interminable circuits around the very limited space in her apartment, as she carried the unhappy bundle that was her baby. A baby who had been fed and changed and cuddled and should have been asleep more than an hour ago.

She'd glanced at the fridge because she was hungry. Hungry enough to wonder if she'd actually remembered to eat at all, today. Oh, yeah... She'd used the last of the peanut butter on the last slice of bread, hadn't she? The plan had been to walk to the nearest supermarket this afternoon to get some more supplies but it hadn't quite happened. The washing machine, tucked under her kitchen bench beside the fridge, had simply stopped working and the repairman had arrived hours later than he'd promised.

And then it was time to feed Jamie again. And give him a bath. She'd had to dip into the emergency supply of disposable nappies because none of the washing that had finally been done had had time to dry yet and Ellie could only hope that the grow suit he was wearing would last until the morning because everything else in her son's meagre wardrobe was either amongst the new load in the washing machine or hanging over the bars of the laundry rack that filled the space between one end of her couch and the television in the corner of her living area.

'Shh…shh…shh…' She rocked the baby as she turned around, stepped past the plastic baby bath that had to get propped up against the kitchen wall because there was no room for it in the bathroom, passed the end of the couch that wasn't obscured by the metal frame of the drying rack and took the ten steps available before she came to her bed.

An unmade bed that looked astonishingly inviting. She could be asleep the moment her head hit that pillow. For an hour or two, anyway, until the small person in the bassinet that had replaced her bedside table woke up again. Even the prospect of being woken was enough for her heart to sink and the threat of tears to surface. This was all so much harder than she had expected.

And so much more lonely…

Ellie hadn't spoken to anyone today, other than the washing machine repairman. Oh, she'd talked to Jamie a lot but that didn't really count as a conversation, did it? This was the longest time ever that she hadn't talked to Ava, she realised. They had always been in some form of contact—almost every day.

The total shock of the surrogacy plan going so wrong had evaporated in those first moments of falling in love with her baby. Ellie had wanted to contact her best friend, in fact, and tell her that it was just as well she didn't want the baby any more because there was no way on earth Ellie could have given him away. She'd actually tried to ring Ava a few days later. Her phone was in the pocket of her jeans right now but there would be no point trying again. Not when the number was no longer valid.

Where was her best friend now? Was she with anyone or nursing her broken heart alone? She should have stayed here and they could have worked things out. Helped each other.

Other friends were here for her but it wasn't like the bond she and Ava had always had. Despite that, Ellie would have been delighted to have a friend like Sue drop in. They could talk about all the exciting cases that had come through the emergency department recently and all the interesting things that were happening in the lives of the people they both knew. But Sue wouldn't be dropping in. Or even ringing. She was working an afternoon shift and wouldn't finish until eleven p.m.

Was Luke still working that shift, too...?

Good grief...was that unpleasant twinge due to envy that Sue might be getting a chance she couldn't have? To work alongside Luke and get to know him a bit better?

No. It was more likely that she was simply missing her work so much. A while back, a few weeks off to prepare for and then recover from giving birth had held all the attraction of an extended holiday but, like the rest of her life, that plan felt as if it had been made by a completely different person who had been living a life that now seemed increasingly like a distant dream.

At least the raucous dinner party in the apartment directly above hers seemed to be winding down. The incessant thumping of feet on her ceiling and the shrieks of drunken laughter hadn't been helping either her mission to settle Jamie into sleep or her emotional state. Other people were having fun. She was becoming a sleep-deprived zombie who spent her nights walking round and round a mind-numbingly restricted track. There was nothing she hadn't seen on this circuit a million times. She had even memorised that phone number on the fridge without even trying.

She had to stop before she fell over from exhaustion. On the next circuit, Ellie slowed down and paused by the end of the couch. Still rocking Jamie, she eased herself onto the edge of the cushion and, when that didn't trigger an increase of misery, she inched back, tucking the baby securely into the crook of her arm, and then relaxed her neck just to let her head rest for a moment on the back of the couch.

Maybe it was her imagination but the cries were lessening in strength. Ellie knew she should get up and have another go at putting Jamie into his bassinet but the command to her legs didn't have any effect.

In a minute, she promised herself. *I'll just close my eyes for a few seconds.* They weren't exactly focusing very well right now so it was weird that she noticed that scrap of paper on the fridge again...

Her mind drifted back in time. Because she was missing the special people in her life so much right now? Ava. And her mother. How much easier would this all be if she still had her mum around to help? To give advice, or help with some of the chores or even take care of the baby and let her get some of that desperately needed sleep.

That sense of loss extended to more than simply family. Memories of growing up in a town small enough to be called a village seemed like a fantasy life now. There was sunshine and the greenery of fields and forests. A beach not that far away. People had time to really care about each other and a new mother would have been showered with help and gifts. Like all those tiny, knitted clothes that her mother's knitting circle had produced.

Had she really rolled her eyes when she got home from school every Wednesday to find that group of women in the living room with their tongues clacking along with their knitting needles? Ellie would sit in the kitchen to do her homework and dream of living in the city where people had more exciting things to do than sit around and gossip.

Jamie was a heavy weight in her arms now and she could recognise the relaxation of tiny muscles that told her he was drifting into a deep sleep. It was definitely time to put him to bed.

But what if he woke up again when she moved?

And besides…there was a new memory floating to the surface of her brain and if she moved, it would vanish.

It was thinking about that knitting circle that had triggered it. About the gossip. She had abandoned her homework that day in order to listen because they were talking about that boy. The new boy who had started catching their bus.

The conversation from so long ago came back in snatches and some of it was more like feelings than actual words but still made sense.

'Taking on a boy that age…?'

'Apparently no foster home could keep him. Too disruptive.'

'Why would the Gilmores do it, then? They're not exactly spring chickens…'

'I know the answer to that. I was talking to Dorothy only the other week…'

The silence of even the knitting needles must have been a satisfying level of attention for the speaker.

'They caught him stealing food. He'd been hiding out in that forest at the back of their place. Eric called the police because he knew someone would want to know where a lad that age was and when Stu arrived with someone from Social Services, Dorothy said she couldn't let them take him away. She said there was something about the way he looked that just broke her heart—as if he'd known all along that there was no hope in the world.'

Ellie had caught her breath at that. Really? The boy on the bus didn't look sad or pathetic. He looked...as if he could take on the world and win—every time.

'Well, he landed on his feet this time, didn't he? Shame he didn't pull his socks up a bit faster.'

'Old habits die hard, I reckon.'

'It's not as if he's breaking any laws.'

'He's a law unto himself, that one. I wouldn't let my daughter anywhere near him, that's for sure and cer-tain.'

Ellie could actually hear that murmur of agreement amongst the women and remember how puzzled she'd been by the odd sound that followed.

Like a collective sigh that wasn't really audible.

She'd been too young to understand it then but now...

She felt the corner of her mouth lift a little. Some things had probably been the same since the dawn of time, hadn't they?

The good girls always denied it—as she had in later years—but it was a thing. That compelling attraction the bad boys often had. Or was it only the bad boys with a charisma that suggested there was something good hidden from sight?

And Luke had been that kind of bad boy. Dorothy Gilmore might have been the first person to see what was hidden but every girl at Kauri Valley District High School was aware of that attraction. Even the ones who knew they would never be chosen.

Like Ellie...

The memories faded. And Ellie's exhaustion seemed to be fading as well as she slipped into a sleep as deep as the baby she was still cradling in her arms.

He was in her dream.

Tall and gorgeous. Wearing faded jeans and a black tee shirt under a battered leather jacket that clung to those broad shoulders like a second skin. She could see the sun streaked golden stripes in that tousled mane of hair. She could feel the surprising softness of it between her fingers as she pushed them over his scalp.

He was smiling down at her—white teeth just visible between lips that were, curiously, soft and firm at exactly the same time. And as delicious as she'd always known they would be.

He was about to kiss her again. She could see it in the glint of his eyes that made the golden flecks against the tawny brown of his irises almost glow.

He was murmuring something. She could see his lips moving but couldn't hear the words but she was smiling. She didn't need to hear them because she could feel his hands on her body and she knew that he was simply telling her about all the things he was about to do to her. Things that she would never, ever be able to forget...

But then his face was changing.

Twisting.

Turning ugly.

And she could hear his words.

'*Get out*…you have to get out of my life… *Now...*'

Somebody was crying. But it didn't sound like her. It was the cry of a child waking. A baby.

And the hands on her body were rough. They were pulling at her. Shaking her hard…

'Wake up…' The voice was louder. 'You have to get out… There's a *fire*… Here… I'll take the baby…'

Ellie's eyes opened in the same instant her brain snapped back into reality.

Or tried to.

She couldn't see properly. The only light in the room was coming from streetlamps several floors below and even that was murky.

Smoky. She could smell it now. Burning and acrid in her nostrils.

She could hear shouts and thumping coming from the apartment above and more shouting from the stairwell beyond her door. Banging on other doors and people yelling for others to wake up and get out.

'*Fire*…the building's on *fire*…'

But the loudest sound of all was the baby crying in her arms as someone tried to pull him out of her grip.

'*No...*' Ellie struggled to sit up. 'Don't take him. He's…' *Mine...* The instinct to protect Jamie was stronger than her own fear but she was forced to stop speaking as she began to cough. She was moving, though. Getting herself up from the couch, grateful for the strong arm gripping her shoulders and shoving her forwards.

She had seen this man before. He lived on the same floor she did but she didn't know his name—this person who had broken through her door to come and save her.

Save *them*...

There were others in the stairwell. Someone other than Jamie was crying now and there were too many people talking at the same time. Shouting to be heard.

'Watch your step.'

'Has someone called the fire brigade?'

'Where's Carla? *Carla?* Can you hear me?'

'Why didn't the damn fire alarm work?'

And then they were outside in the dark and the shocking reality was lit up against the night sky. Flames licked the building, coming from the windows only a floor above Ellie's apartment.

Where the party had been happening.

The sound of glass shattering was accompanied by billows of smoke coming from higher windows and then more flames joined the image until there was a solid wall of flames moving upwards.

And sirens... The emergency services were arriving. A police car and then the first of many fire trucks. An ambulance. People in uniforms were herding the crowd of residents further and further away from the building until they were right at the end of the block. More ambulances were rolling up, their lights flashing against the darkness of the night. A television crew arrived, spilling out of the branded four-by-four and lifting cameras to their shoulders even as they moved towards the scene. Someone was stringing bright tape across the road so they couldn't go back. There were hoses being unravelled and ladders being raised and the noise levels were increasing steadily.

So much shouting.

Ellie was wedged into the crowd, holding Jamie as if her own life depended on keeping him safe. Horrified by the thought that she could still be in that building—unconscious now instead of simply asleep—because she would have had no warning of the deadly smoke rolling in beneath her door. She looked around at her silent neighbours, who were simply standing there, watching their homes being destroyed, trying to find the man who had saved her so that she could thank him properly.

But someone in a uniform was in the way.

'Come with us, love.' The paramedic was putting a blanket around Ellie's shoulders. 'We need to check you and your baby.'

Her baby...

It had seemed extraordinary that Jamie had gone back to sleep in her arms as she stood there rocking him. But was he really only asleep? There had been enough smoke to make her cough. What would that have done to tiny airways and lungs? The relief of being outside and safe was obliterated by fear again as Ellie let the paramedics guide her into the back of the nearest ambulance.

They checked heart-rates and blood pressure and oxygen saturation levels. They listened to Ellie's lung sounds, making her take deep breaths that made her cough. The stethoscope looked huge against Jamie's little chest and he woke up and began to cry again.

But he wasn't coughing.

'He seems fine,' the paramedic told her. 'But we can take you into Emergency for a full check if you're worried. Did you say he's only three weeks old? It might be a good idea to go to hospital.'

But Ellie knew that cry. Jamie was hungry.

'I'll just feed him, if that's okay…and then see how he is…'

'Sure. Stay in here where it's warm. We've got enough trucks to transport anybody that's urgent.' She lifted the back of the stretcher and put pillows behind Ellie so that she could sit more comfortably as she settled Jamie against her breast. 'I know you, don't I?' The paramedic was focused on Ellie's face now, instead of a detailed physical assessment. 'Do you work at North Shore General?'

'I did. I'm on maternity leave.'

'Of course…' The paramedic smiled down at Jamie. 'He's gorgeous.' She shook her head. 'I can't imagine how scary that must have been. Were you asleep when the fire started?'

Ellie nodded. Sound asleep. Dreaming about…

No…she couldn't remember. And it didn't matter. All that mattered was that they were both safe. Unharmed. Jamie was sucking steadily, his eyes drifting shut, and the snuffling sounds he was making were perfectly normal with no hint of any respiratory distress. Had being wrapped in his blanket and cuddled against her chest saved him from inhaling a significant amount of that evil smoke?

The paramedic had opened the back door of the ambulance and was leaning out. The cacophony of sound from outside sounded like a disaster movie. Something Ellie had been watching but didn't affect her. She looked down at the tiny face against her breast and the first wave of real relief washed over her. She could feel tears rolling down her face.

'Oh, my God...' The paramedic sounded awed. 'It looks like the building's collapsing in the middle...'

And then it hit Ellie.

She had nothing but the precious baby in her arms and the clothes she was wearing. Sneakers. A pair of maternity jeans and an ancient, sloppy tee shirt that had a red bird with an open beak and a cloud of tiny hearts emerging instead of musical notes for its song.

She had been frightened of how she was going to cope when she knew she had a baby to take home and she didn't have as much as a single nappy.

Now she didn't even have a home.

She needed help right now, more than she ever had.

And, of course, the first person who came to mind was Ava.

But there was no point in trying. She'd known that when she'd thought about it earlier. When she'd been aware of the lump of her phone in her back pocket as she'd been walking that track round and round her apartment.

Such a small, inadequate space to be looking after a baby but it had been home.

Their home.

She could see the last glimpses of it that she would ever have. The clothes rack with the laundry drying. The bassinet beside her unmade bed. The fridge...

The fridge with that scrap of paper half hidden by the smiley face magnet.

With the number that she knew by heart.

Was her phone still in her pocket or had it slipped out during that frantic escape of getting up from the couch and through the smoke filled corridor, down what had felt like endless flights of concrete stairs and then further and further along the road?

Trying not to disturb Jamie's sleepy, contented sucking, Ellie moved one arm, snaking her hand towards her pocket.

There'd been no traffic to speak of at this time of night but it was still a bit of a drive all the way to Kauri Valley and Luke hadn't felt ready to sleep. He'd opened a cold beer, and fired up his laptop to look up a journal article he'd thought of earlier this evening. It had been written by the person who currently led the team in the emergency department of the hospital in Boston he was about to put an application in to work with. He wanted to know how good their research program was.

A news alert popped up and, without thinking, he clicked on it to find himself watching a live feed of breaking news. An old multi-storey apartment block in one of the North Shore suburbs close to the hospital was being engulfed in fire.

Luke pushed his barely tasted beer away. Were there casualties? Would he be called in to help with an unexpected influx of patients?

Almost as the thought occurred to him, his mobile started ringing.

But it was the last person he would have expected it to be on the other end of the line.

'Luke? It's Ellie Thomas...'

Ellie...

Luke's mouth suddenly felt weirdly dry. 'Hey, Ellie...' was all he could manage.

'You...um...you gave me your number. The night Jamie was born?'

Luke nodded and then realised how stupid that was. 'Yeah. I did.' Something in Ellie's tone was making coherent thought difficult. She sounded...frightened? No...more like *lost*...

He could hear a lot of background noise, too. Shouting. And a distant siren. Where on earth was she at this time of night? And what about the baby? A sudden chill ran up his spine. Had something happened to Jamie?

'You said if I ever needed help...' Oh, God...she was crying. He could hear the catch of her breath that sounded like a stifled sob. 'I think... I need help...'

CHAPTER FOUR

'Are you sure about this?'

'Of course. I wouldn't have offered, otherwise.'

Luke glanced sideways at the passenger in his car. Ellie still had the ambulance blanket around her shoulders. Her hair was a bit of a mess, with those tangled, dark blonde waves framing a pale face that was smudged with dark streaks. He was pretty sure it must have been her tears that had left cleaner patches on the layer of soot from the smoke.

He knew she was only two years younger than his own thirty-four years because he'd seen it written in her hospital notes. But right now, she looked more than ten years younger—almost like the young girl who used to share his school bus, except that he would have noticed her back then, if she'd ever looked *this* miserable. Ellie also looked exhausted and more than a little frightened and those huge, dark eyes in that pale face were so striking that Luke had to force his gaze back to the road. The expression in them made her look incredibly vulnerable and it made his heart ache in a way that he couldn't put a name to, with a strength that was oddly disturbing.

'And are you sure you don't want to get checked out at hospital? Or have Jamie checked again?'

She nodded. 'I've just got a bit of airway irritation from the smoke.' Her cough punctuated her words with perfect timing. 'I'll be fine. Just a bit shocked, I guess. Jamie doesn't even have a cough and he's too young to have been really frightened. He's fine, too, and that's all that really matters.'

Luke might have disagreed with that but couldn't think of how he could say so without it sounding strange coming from someone who didn't even qualify as a friend. Yet...

He simply nodded and concentrated on his driving, instead. Offering Ellie a place to stay for the night had been the most obvious way he could provide the help that had been requested of him and he *had* been sure. He couldn't remember ever having wanted to help someone in trouble quite this much, in fact. Being able to do this had wiped out that unsettling knowledge that had come with that conversation with Sue tonight—the unfairness of life that had him rattling around alone in a huge old house while Ellie was caring for a baby in no more than a bedsit. It wasn't just for Ellie's, sake, of course. He still felt that odd connection with the baby he'd thought might be just as unwanted as he had once been.

He turned his head enough to glance into the back seat, now. He could see that Jamie was fast asleep in the plastic capsule with the handle. 'We were lucky that ambulance crew had a baby car seat they could lend us.'

'They know where we work. Where *you* work, any-way...' There was a note in Ellie's voice that made Luke wonder just how much she was missing her job in the ED. 'Any crew will be able to collect the seat and the blanket and return them.'

Luke flicked on his indicator. 'There's an all-night

service station here. We can go shopping properly to-morrow, but what do you need most now?'

Ellie closed her eyes and Luke caught the tremble of her lips as she obviously started to itemise everything she had just lost. Again, his heart squeezed with that nameless emotion. It squeezed so hard he could feel a lump in his own throat.

Her voice, however, came out with a surprising level of determination. She wasn't beaten, yet, this young mother. With her first words, he could identify what he was feeling this time. He was proud of her. He'd al-ready known she had guts when she'd embraced the challenge of raising a child she hadn't intended to bring into the world. Now, she was demonstrating that she wasn't going to let anything stop her. Even the trauma of watching her home get destroyed.

'Nappies,' she said. 'And baby wipes. Clothes might be a problem but a service station isn't going to stock them.' She bit her lip. 'I don't have any money with me, though. My wallet got left behind.'

'It's not a problem.'

'I'll pay you back. As soon as I can sort things. Oh, help... I don't even have any ID for going to the bank.' With a despairing groan, Ellie faltered, burying her face in her hands. 'I can't believe this has happened...'

Luke pulled into a parking space in front of the ser-vice station. He put his hand on Ellie's shoulder in what was meant to be simply a reassuring touch but when he felt how rigid she was with tension he extended his fingers and gave it a slow squeeze.

'It'll be okay,' he told her. 'We can sort everything—one step at a time. You stay here with Jamie. I reckon

I can manage to find the right sort of disposable nappies and wipes.'

Ellie's face appeared and the look in her eyes made Luke feel about ten feet tall. A knight in shining armour who still had the damsel in distress on the back of his horse. And he could feel her skin, even through the layers of the blanket and her tee shirt, sending tendrils of warmth that made his arm and then his whole body tingle.

'New born size for the nappies.' She was trying to smile but it wobbled. 'And the wipes with aloe vera are really good, if they've got them.'

He came back with his arms laden with what looked like enough nappies and wipes to last for at least a week and a smile that suggested triumph.

A smile that made him look like that teenaged boy she could remember getting onto the school bus—with the kind of swagger that told everybody there wasn't anything he couldn't handle and he was going to have fun with whatever challenge got thrown at him.

A 'bad boy' kind of smile.

And it was impossible not to smile back.

Impossible not to feel as if, with this man's help, Ellie could face anything. Even when she was feeling as if she were falling into a black hole in her life that she'd never seen coming.

He'd already brought her through the worst moments of her life when she'd been afraid that she could lose the lives of both her baby and herself.

Maybe that was why she hadn't even thought to call Sue or another friend to ask for help tonight.

She'd felt so lost, sitting there in the back of that ambulance with Jamie in her arms, knowing she had lost her home and all her possessions. Even her car had been parked in the basement of the apartment block and had undoubtedly been buried under the collapsed building.

And she'd remembered that moment when Luke had crouched beside her in the emergency department to ask for her consent to let him take charge of her assisted delivery. When she'd looked into his eyes and found hope to cling to.

And when, in that grim time of the pain and the pushing, he had called her 'sweetheart'...

So she had to smile back now. He was doing exactly what she'd hoped he would. Taking charge of an unexpected and horrible moment and giving her the confidence that she could, actually, cope with this.

'Step one sorted,' he said with satisfaction as he started the car again. 'Now let's get you home.'

Ellie had to swallow a big lump in her throat.

She didn't have a home any more.

But, weirdly, as they left the motorway and headed west, it *felt* as if she were heading home. She knew this country like the back of her hand, with its rolling hills and paddocks shaded by so many trees and the small village with its town hall and war memorial and the pub on the main street.

'I haven't been out to Kauri Valley in years,' she murmured. 'There didn't seem any point after Mum died.'

'Same.' Luke nodded. 'It was five years ago that my dad died and when it became obvious that Mum needed full time care, I moved her to Sydney so she'd be close enough for me to help take care of her.'

Ellie was struck by his choice of words. And the tone

with which he used them. If you didn't know, you'd never guess that he'd been adopted so late in his childhood. He was talking about his family, here. A family he had loved very much.

And lost.

Ellie had lost her family, too.

She had lost her best friend.

She had lost her future as she'd envisioned it.

Now she had lost her home.

It was all too much. And hearing that note of such caring in Luke's voice brought tears to her eyes again. She sniffed hard as she tried to blink them away.

Luke's glance was swift.

'You okay?'

Oh, man… He still sounded as though he cared so much, but this time it was on her behalf. Ellie had to close her eyes. Just for a heartbeat, she wanted to feel as if that concern were genuinely personal. That someone really cared.

'Mmm. I just… I can tell how special your mum was to you. And… I was missing *my* mum tonight. And now, it feels like I'm heading home, even though that's crazy.'

Luke was silent for a moment. A moment of empathy for someone else who had no family?

Or maybe he understood how weird it felt to be entering such an old stamping ground again.

'It hasn't changed much,' he said. 'Kauri Valley, that is. Mr Jenkins still runs the general store.' His tone was cheerful now. Was he trying to distract her from thinking too much about her current problems? 'Do you remember him?'

'But he was ancient twenty years ago! And so

grumpy. He thought that kids only came into his shop to steal lollies.'

Luke's mouth twitched. 'Maybe some of them did.'

Ellie's jaw dropped. Okay. She had been very effectively distracted.

'You *didn't*...' But then she bit her lip. 'Actually, Ava and I did, once, too. Just to see if we could... And because he was shouting at someone's dog who'd snuck in the door and the poor dog was cringing as if it was getting beaten.'

'Did you get away with it?'

'Yes...but we felt so guilty we never did it again.'

'Mmm.'

There was a world of understanding in that sound. Had it been guilt that had finally put Lucas Gilmore on a straight and narrow path? Did you only feel guilty when you were scared of being punished? Or was it because you cared about what other people thought? That only mattered when you cared about those people, didn't it?

Ellie stole a sideways glance at Luke. It wasn't the first time she had wondered about what life had been like for him as a child. How he had ended up hiding in the forest behind the Gilmores' place. Part of his charisma had come from the shroud of mystery he'd brought with him into a very ordinary New Zealand high school, but after Ellie had eavesdropped on that conversation between the group of local women, something else had captured her imagination.

How he'd come to look as if he'd believed there was no hope in the world.

Forgetting her own worries for a moment longer, Ellie felt something in her heart squeeze very tightly, as if she could see that young boy looking so desperate that he had touched Dorothy Gilmore's heart enough to make her change her life for ever. And then she had to twist her head to look at Jamie, asleep in the car seat. She would never let anything bad happen to him.

But it almost had tonight...

Maybe it was delayed shock that was making her shiver as they finally pulled into a driveway that was so overgrown, the hedges scraped the sides of the SUV. The screeching sound woke Jamie, who began to whimper as Luke unbuckled the plastic capsule. The shivering was almost shaking by the time she had followed him up some wide steps, across a veranda with creaking boards and through a front door that led into the widest, longest hallway Ellie had ever seen. Finally, having led her into a kitchen that was probably bigger than her entire apartment had been, Luke put down the pile of nappies and wipes he had under one arm, and carefully put down the baby seat containing Jamie he'd been carrying in his other hand.

One glance at Ellie and he frowned so deeply he almost looked angry.

'You're frozen... Here...' He was stripping off the woollen, ribbed jumper he was wearing. 'Put this on.'

It was massive. And still warm from his body.

It felt like a hug.

And it smelled...delicious. Ellie couldn't help crossing her arms and bringing them up to her face so that she could bury her nose in the scent for a moment. She was watching Luke at the same time, as he dropped to a crouch in front of the baby seat and rocked it a little.

'It's okay, little guy,' he said. 'Do you want to come out of this? Do you need your mummy?'

He had been wearing a black tee shirt under the jumper and, right now, it was stretched against the muscles of his back and shoulders.

And, suddenly, Ellie remembered what she had been dreaming about when she'd been shaken awake by her neighbour. Worse, she could actually feel fingers of remembered desire curling themselves into a tight fist somewhere deep in her belly as her gaze travelled down his bare arms to those large hands with long, artistic looking fingers.

Why had her subconscious chosen to give her a sex dream about Luke Gilmore, for heaven's sake? Had it become bored with the smudged features of the purely fantasy partners that had entered her dreams on the odd occasion during more than a year of celibacy?

Oh…help…

It wasn't just the new item of clothing making her feel so much warmer. Her cheeks felt as if they had started glowing. At least Luke had his back to her so he couldn't have noticed anything and she had to make sure he never did. He would be horrified. She had been on another planet at school as far as his sexual interests were concerned and there was no reason to believe something that fundamental would have changed. How embarrassing would it be if he thought that was the reason she had called him tonight?

It wasn't.

Or was it? Trusting someone, not to mention liking how they could make you feel by simply looking at you, had to be a big part of attraction.

But feelings that were unmistakeably sexual were on a whole different—and very inappropriate—level. She was just exhausted, Ellie reminded herself. She'd been through an emotional mill tonight. And it was probably far too long since she'd had a man in her life.

With an effort, Ellie got a grip.

'I'll get him,' she told Luke. 'He probably needs feeding again.'

'Oh...of course... What do you need?' He looked around. 'Those kitchen chairs aren't very comfortable but the living room will be pretty cold—I don't use it much.'

'That couch looks perfect.' Ellie unbuckled Jamie's safety belt and picked up the baby, supporting the back of his head with one hand as she lifted him to her shoulder. It was automatic to turn her head enough to kiss the soft fluff of his hair. 'I've never seen a kitchen big enough to have a couch in it before.'

'It's always been the heart of the house.' Luke spoke quietly. 'My favourite room. I used to do my guitar practice on that couch while Mum was cooking dinner. She said she liked to have music while she worked.'

Ellie didn't say anything. Maybe because she was trying not to picture a teenaged Luke, with even longer, shaggier hair and a guitar in his arms. He would have totally owned a rock star vibe. Trying to distract herself, she focused on the room, instead.

On the old beams in the ceiling and the stone floor and the scuffed looking leather of the big couch. There were French doors to one side of the couch but it was too dark to see anything more than an area of stone paving, notable for the tall weeds filling the gaps between the big, flat stones. And one of the big windows on either side of the doors had tape criss-crossed over a large crack.

Luke noticed what had caught her attention as she

was sitting down. He walked towards the window and ran his fingers over the tape.

'The place is a bit run down still. The rental firm I was using let me down and I arrived back to find a complete mess. It's clean now, though. The commercial cleaners I got in even washed all the linen and aired mattresses.'

He had his hand on the door knob now. Turning it to check that it was locked. 'It's safe, too. I had all the locks changed. Someone's coming to fix the windows and some other stuff soon. I just need to find a gardener that doesn't take one look and either say he's too busy or give me a ridiculous quote because they don't actually want the work.'

He turned just in time to see Ellie guiding Jamie's gaping little mouth to help him latch on to her nipple. She could feel the way he seemed to freeze for a heartbeat. And then another.

'I...ah... I'll put the kettle on, shall I? Would you like a cup of tea or coffee or something?'

'A cup of tea would be awesome. But don't let me keep you up. It's the middle of the night and you've got work tomorrow.'

'I've got a day off tomorrow.' He filled an electric jug and switched it on and then, without looking in Ellie's direction again, he hurried out of the kitchen, muttering something about finding linen for her bed.

Anyone would think he'd never seen a woman breastfeeding her baby before, Ellie thought. For heaven's sake...he'd told her that he'd done a long stint in obstetrics. He must be more than used to the sight of a woman's breast, not to mention every other part of their anatomy.

Or was he uncomfortable because it was *her* breast he had glimpsed?

Because he saw her as a woman and not a patient?

Maybe something had changed in the years since she had been an invisible teenager. He had, after all, told her that she was *special…*

That thought merged with remnants of desire that were still glowing deep inside and made her toes curl more than a little but Ellie was still confused.

When Luke had given up doing the kind of things that would get him expelled from school, like playing truant or smoking behind the bike sheds, he'd found a new 'bad boy' niche at Kauri Valley High—as the resident heartbreaker.

And it didn't seem to matter how many hearts got broken, there was always another girl fighting to get to the front of the queue. She and Ava used to whisper about it on the bus.

'Did you hear that Charlene got dumped?'

'Yeah…but nobody lasts more than two or three dates, do they?'

'Who's next, do you reckon?'

'Dunno…that redheaded girl, maybe. The one who gets into trouble all the time for wearing her skirt too short. What's her name… Tegan?'

She couldn't remember any more of the legendary pack of Gilmore girlfriends but it was clear that Luke would be quite familiar with breasts in both his professional and personal life.

So it was weird that he had seemed uncomfortable.

Unless he was regretting his decision to bring her home? Maybe he didn't really trust her yet, despite that curiously intimate chat they'd had on the night of Jamie's birth. She had, after all, announced that nobody wanted the baby she had just given birth to—including herself.

The memory still made her wince. And cuddle Jamie a little bit closer.

'It wasn't true,' she whispered. 'It will never be true.'

He had finished feeding. She lifted him upright and began to rub his back to burp him, tilting her head so that she could feel his hair against her cheek. Despite the weariness that was coming back in a tidal wave and the fact that life had just thrown her another rather dramatic curveball, she found herself singing softly. The old Brahms lullaby that had become a familiar part of this routine in just a few, short weeks.

Sleepyhead, close your eyes, for I'm right beside you...

Luke could hear the song well before he reached the kitchen, with a stack of clean towels in his arms. This old, isolated house was so quiet, you could just about hear a mouse scratching in the pantry at this time of night.

Ellie had a beautiful voice. He recognised the tune, of course. Who hadn't heard that old lullaby that seemed to be part of every mobile that new parents hung over a baby's bassinet? It had always struck him as being a bit mournful but maybe that was because he'd never lost the sense of yearning for something he'd probably never had.

A mother's love...

He'd learned to wall it off. So effectively it barely touched his consciousness so it had been a shock when he'd felt it so strongly only a short time ago, when he'd seen Ellie beginning to feed her baby.

And now it was happening again, as he listened to the soft sound of her song.

There was something about this particular mother and child that touched a part of him that he had considered insignificant now. Okay, he'd had an unfortunate start in life but he'd overcome it, thanks to the Gilmores. He was an adult. An extremely successful adult who had everything he could want in life—an exciting job, no financial worries and the freedom to go anywhere he chose in the world.

He didn't want to be reminded of things he had never had when he was young. Or the things that were impossible for him to have now.

Like a family...

Had it been a mistake to bring Ellie and Jamie into the only place that felt like a family home to him?

Ah well...it was only for a night. He could help them find somewhere else to go tomorrow.

Taking a deep breath, he entered the kitchen and put the towels down on the big, wooden table in the centre of the room. Ellie stopped singing as soon as she saw him come into the room and she was well covered with his old jumper again so it was easy to sound perfectly relaxed.

'Your bed's all sorted. I didn't know what to do for Jamie, though. Can he sleep in the car seat?'

'Oh... I guess so. Or I can keep him in the bed with me.'

Luke frowned. Co-sleeping with an infant was controversial. Some suggested it was less than safe but if that was what Ellie wanted to do, it was her decision. He busied himself making the tea but the urge to suggest that the plan was unwise gained momentum. As he put two mugs onto the table, inspiration struck.

'I saw a movie, once,' he said. 'Some baby got born unexpectedly in an old house and they made a bed for it in a big drawer from the bottom of a Scotch chest.'

'Oh?' Ellie was walking towards the table. She tucked Jamie securely under one arm and reached for the mug of tea with her other hand.

'I've got a Scotch chest in my room and half the drawers are empty.'

She was looking at the towels. 'They'd probably make a good mattress, wouldn't they?'

'I'll go and get the drawer.'

He was back in less than a minute. He put the old, wooden drawer on the table and covered its base—not with the towels but with the folded hospital blanket that Ellie didn't need any more. Then he put a clean towel on the top.

Ellie laid Jamie gently into the nest and tucked him in with another towel. He scrunched up his face and stretched tiny, starfish hands above his head but then relaxed back into sleep.

Ellie smiled up at Luke. 'I'm liking the Kiwi ingenuity,' she said. 'And thanks, Luke. For...' She looked as if she had a whole bunch of things she wanted to say but couldn't decide where to begin. The way her gaze slid away from his suggested embarrassment and reminded him of the shy girl she had been way back. 'For everything.'

Man...those eyes...that smile...and that little wobble in her voice that told him how much this meant to her.

What was it about Ellie Thomas that seemed so astonishingly different from any woman he had ever met?

He found himself willing her to look back and catch his gaze again. He wanted to smile back at her.

No. What he really wanted to do was gather her into his arms and just hold her. To reassure that shy Ellie enough that brave Ellie came back.

Okay. That wasn't entirely true, either.

He wanted...

He wanted...to *kiss* her.

The realisation was shocking.

He had brought this exhausted, vulnerable brand-new mother into his home in the wake of a personal disaster. Of course she was grateful. To even think of taking advantage of that in any way was appalling.

Any man would find Ellie Thomas attractive but the last thing she needed in her life at the moment was someone who was even entertaining the idea of hitting on her.

What she needed right now was a friend.

A big brother.

A very long time ago Luke had made a promise to the amazing woman who'd chosen to become his mother that he would always strive to be the best person that he could possibly be, however hard that was.

Putting Ellie Thomas completely off limits wasn't actually that hard because it was the right thing to do.

The only thing to do.

Luke turned away. 'Let me show you your room. You bring your tea. I'll bring Jamie.'

The big wooden drawer with the baby asleep inside it was a lot heavier than a bassinet would have been.

And rather more awkward to hold but Luke tucked it under his arm, confident that Jamie was perfectly safe.

So was Ellie.

He'd make sure of that.

CHAPTER FIVE

HE'D GONE CRAZY.

But Ellie had been forced to stop trying to moderate Luke's behaviour thirty minutes ago.

'We'll talk about that later,' he'd said, with a hint of impatience at having to repeat himself so often. 'Stop worrying, Ellie—I've got this.' He leaned closer so that he could whisper in her ear. 'To tell you the truth, I haven't had this much fun in a very long time.'

The glint in his eyes told her that he meant what he said. The low growl of his voice so close to her ear that it tickled made Ellie feel as if something were melting deep inside her. The something that controlled the muscles in her legs, maybe? At least the need to sit down for a bit became a priority when Jamie helpfully decided that he was starving.

Which was hardly surprising. They'd been on a mission for hours now as Luke had helped her launch the sorting out process.

It had taken a bit of time for the bank to cancel the automatic debit for her rent, withdraw some of the remaining cash from her account and arrange for an emergency credit card that would be couriered to her in the next day or two. The police required a statement and she was able to tell them that yes, there had been a party going on in the apartment above her—on the floor where the fire had apparently started—and it *had* sounded a bit out of control. She was given information about emergency housing available through Social Services but it was in a part of the city that made her heart sink and Luke's face scrunch into that angry sort of scowl.

The insurance company had been sympathetic but warned that the process could be slow. And it was only her car that had been insured. Had she not been advised to take out insurance on her personal belongings?

And now, here they were, in the Baby Supermarket and the sales girls had all fallen under Luke's spell the moment he smiled at them.

'We have a little problem,' he'd told them. 'I don't know if you heard about the big fire on the North Shore last night but little Jamie here has been left with nothing but the nappies we picked up last night. We kind of need...*everything*.'

It seemed as if every staff member this huge shop employed had wanted to be part of the most exciting cause to have ever come through their doors. Even the manager had come to see what was going on.

'We'll give you the best discount we can manage,' he told Luke. 'And then take another ten per cent off on top of that. It's the least we can do to help. My word... I saw that fire on the news this morning. Wasn't there a fatality? It must have been terrifying for you both.'

If Luke had noticed the assumption that was being made, he didn't try and correct it. Maybe because he seemed to be fascinated by how much was clearly essential for looking after a tiny baby.

'A change table—so that's what this is?'

'Fully washable surface.' A girl with bright red streaks in her hair was clearly delighted to have captured Luke's attention. 'There's the shelves here to keep supplies like nappies and towels and these drawers are for creams and wipes. And look...the top is really a lid that covers where the bath clips in.'

'Do you like it?' Luke asked Ellie.

She was already a bit stunned by what was going on. 'It's amazing. But, Luke, I—'

'We'll take it,' Luke said. 'What's next?'

The bassinet, apparently. And bedding. A state-of-the-art car seat. A front pack and baby sling. They were nowhere near the numerous aisles stacked with cloth nappies and clothing and toys but Jamie's cries were getting louder.

'Let me show you our mothers' area.' A senior staff member smiled at Ellie. 'Here at the Baby Supermarket, we pride ourselves on making our mothers and babies feel right at home. Are you breastfeeding, dear?'

Ellie nodded.

'Then come with me. We have change facilities and a private feeding room. There's a rocking chair in there that is unbelievably comfortable.' Her glance slid back towards Luke as she led Ellie away. 'It's on special, too, with a twenty-five per cent discount—just for today...'

It was a good thing that Luke didn't follow her because he would probably have added one of these chairs to the scary pile of purchases being piled up near one of the check-out counters.

Even the soothing motion of the rocking chair couldn't stop Ellie's level of anxiety rising as she took the time necessary to feed Jamie. This shopping spree was going to cost hundreds, if not thousands of dollars. How on earth could she possibly pay him back when she wasn't even working again yet?

And, given the helpful advice of all those attractive young women, just how crazy was Luke going to go in the clothing aisles?

Judging by the large bags that were being packed by the time she emerged from the mothers and babies' retreat, he hadn't held back. And when had he added that pushchair to the pile? It wasn't even an ordinary pushchair. It was one of those expensive three-wheeled mountain buggies that Ellie would never have dreamed of budgeting for.

He'd already paid for everything, too. And the manager was practically rubbing his hands together.

'We can offer free and immediate delivery.'

'That won't be necessary. I've got a Jeep out in the car park. I'm sure we can pack it all in the back.'

Jamie's return distracted the cluster of people around the check-out counter.

'He's so *cute*...' the girls cooed.

Even the most senior woman was looking misty-eyed. She looked from Jamie to Ellie and then Luke.

'He looks just like his daddy,' she said. 'You must be so proud of him.'

For just a heartbeat, Ellie let herself imagine what it would be like if Luke were actually Jamie's father and they'd been here as a family.

Pure fantasy but it was a beautiful thing...

Until Luke's mouth opened and then closed again as his gaze flicked to meet Ellie's. She could see the flash of something like horror as he finally caught on to the assumption everyone had made when they'd arrived here as a couple with their new born baby.

Was he going to tell everyone here that Jamie wasn't his child? That Ellie was nothing more than an acquaintance from long ago? A bus buddy? Maybe he didn't need to say anything. He was looking, for all the world, as if the idea of having a family of his own could possibly be his worst nightmare.

But nobody else had seen what she'd seen and he didn't say anything out loud to shatter the illusion. He seemed as stunned as Ellie had been when this mammoth spend-up had gained momentum.

'We'd better get going,' was all he said. 'Can we get some help taking this lot out to the car park, please?'

Sorting the jigsaw of fitting everything into the back of his Jeep was almost enough to distract Luke from what had just happened.

Almost...

He could understand why it had happened. He and Ellie were pretty much the same age and they were out with a brand-new baby. He hadn't been unaware of the looks he was getting from all the girls and, on some level, maybe he'd known he could enjoy the attention because they assumed he was unavailable and nobody was going to take any flirting the wrong way. To top it off, like a good, old-fashioned husband, he had handed over his credit card and paid for everything.

And then Ellie had come back, with Jamie asleep in her arms looking like an advertisement for a perfect baby and the look on her face as everybody cooed over Jamie had been...

So proud. So full of love...

He'd been watching them, caught up in the moment of admiring this recent addition to the human race, so that comment that put him into a pair of new father's shoes had blindsided him.

Just for a heartbeat, he had known what it would feel like. To have a partner as gorgeous as Ellie and a baby they had created together. A baby he *did* feel absurdly proud of for that split second. And it had felt...

Amazing.

Like the best thing that could happen to anyone. Ever.

It also felt as if one of the foundation stones he'd built his life on had just been blown up and disintegrated from beneath his feet and he was in grave danger of falling into a place that had never even been an option to visit.

Doing something practical, like loading the ridiculous amount of stuff he'd just purchased into his vehicle, was exactly what he needed to climb back into a safe emotional space. He had checked another thing off the list that was sorting out the disaster that Ellie had found herself in.

He was fixing things.

'Next stop, North Shore General,' he said, climbing into the driver's seat. 'We'll drop off that ambulance blanket and car seat.'

The silence in the car started to feel a little awkward. Was Ellie also thinking about that assumption the staff of the Baby Supermarket had made?

Had she—even for that tiny moment of time— thought about what it would be like if it *had* been true?

Something like alarm prickled in Luke's spine. He'd already overstepped a boundary or two becoming in-

volved with someone who had actually been his patient.
Okay, it was a grey area because, although Ellie was on
leave, they were, theoretically, colleagues in the same
department. And they had a childhood connection even
though that was a bit distant. Some boundaries, however, had to be identified.

He couldn't let her imagine that he was offering anything more than the practical assistance that someone
in trouble was in need of. And yeah…he was going a
bit above and beyond and that was his own fault but he
had saved this baby's life, after all. Even if nobody knew
about his own start in life, they wouldn't be surprised
that this little boy had touched his heart in a special way.

But it seemed as if something entirely different was
bothering Ellie.

'I'll pay you back,' she said, finally. 'Every cent.
With interest, even.'

'That's not necessary.'

She shook her head. 'Of course it is. You've already
done far more than most people would for someone
they barely know.'

Luke said nothing. This was good. Ellie was setting
some boundaries herself and declaring them to be almost strangers. He should feel relieved.

So why did he feel kind of…disappointed?

'It might take a wee while, though. I hope that won't
be a problem.'

Luke shook his head. Of course it wasn't a problem.

'I'm not sure how soon I can get back to work,' Ellie
continued. 'I'll have to find good childcare.' Something
like a huff of laughter broke her words. 'Good grief…
I'll have to find somewhere to live, first…'

'There's no rush,' Luke heard himself saying. 'You're

welcome to stay at my place for a few days if it's not too far out of town.'

A voice in the back of his head was making incredulous noises. Reminding him that he'd been relieved that he'd only have to ignore any attraction to this woman for one night. What did he think he was doing?

'Really?' Ellie sounded astonished. 'That would be *awesome*. And the insurance company said they'd approve a rental car so the distance wouldn't matter. I could still get out to view places.'

They wouldn't be spending that much time together, would they? Ellie would be out hunting for a new apartment. He'd be at work a lot of the time.

All he needed now was to firm up those boundaries—for both their sakes.

'And don't worry about paying me back for the baby stuff.' He kept his gaze firmly on the task of locating his designated space on the far side of the North Shore General's car park. 'It sounds like I'm going to get a lot more than I expected when the property sells. I don't have any dependants and I don't intend to get saddled with any, either. Consider it a gift.'

Easing the big vehicle to a stop between the designated lines, he turned his head to offer a smile that would confirm that it was no big deal. That he could afford it easily enough for it to mean virtually nothing.

To his surprise, Ellie was scowling at him. She looked...as disappointed as he'd been when she'd declared them to be no more than strangers?

'I asked for your help,' she said quietly. 'Not charity.'

It was another awkward moment, during which Luke realised how patronising he must have sounded. No wonder Ellie was on the defensive. That flash of anger in her eyes suggested that she would fight for her independence with the same kind of passion that she would use to protect her son.

He had to respect that...

And he needed to apologise.

Luke opened his mouth to do exactly that but, before he could say a word, another sound was heard.

A shriek of extreme pain.

They were still staring at each other so Luke could see the way they both dismissed any thoughts of anything personal. The professional switch had been flipped at precisely the same instant.

'Oh, my God...' Ellie breathed. 'That sounds like a child.'

Luke had his door open already. 'Where did it come from?'

Ellie was out of the car now, too. 'There...look...'

Almost opposite them, a car had stopped at an angle that cut across two parking spaces. The driver's door was open. So was one of the back doors. A woman was reaching into the car and another shriek split the air.

'Nooo... Don't *touch...'*

'I have to, darling... I'm *sorry...'* The woman sounded nearly as upset as the child.

'Nooo...' The shrieks increased in volume. This child was clearly terrified.

Jamie was still sound asleep in his flash, new car seat. Leaving the door open would mean that Ellie could hear him the moment he woke and the vehicle the screaming was coming from was only a few metres away. She didn't hesitate to follow Luke.

'What's wrong?' she heard him ask the woman. 'I'm

one of the doctors from the emergency department.' A quick glance over his shoulder told him that Ellie was right behind him. 'And this is Ellie, one of our nurses.'

'It's Mia—my daughter.' The woman straightened, turning to face Luke. 'We were at the park and she fell out of a tree.' She tried, and failed, to stop her face crumpling and a sob emerging. 'There's something wrong with her arm. I think she's broken it.'

'How high was the tree? And did you see how she landed? Did she hit her head as well?'

Ellie stepped past them, as the mother was answering Luke's questions, into the small gap by the open door. She crouched down so that her head was a little lower than the girl, who had subsided into quieter sobs now that no one was threatening to touch her.

'Hey, Mia… I'm Ellie.'

'Go away…'

'I like your shoes.' Ellie made it sound as if the sneakers were the most exciting thing she'd seen all day. 'Are they the ones that have the sparkly lights when you walk?'

Mia said nothing. She was still glaring at Ellie suspiciously.

'I want a pair of those.' Ellie sighed. 'But they don't make them for big girls like me. How old are you, Mia? Four?'

'No.' Mia was offended enough to be distracted from her fears. 'I'm *five*.'

'Wow…you're going to school already?'

Mia nodded proudly and Ellie smiled at her. She let her gaze slide down as she did so, though. The little girl had one arm cradled against her chest and she was using her other hand to hold it still. Ellie could see the unusual shape of the small elbow on the injured side. She could also see the colour of the hand below it.

'Oh...look at your nail polish... What a pretty colour. I *love* pink... It's my absolutely favourite colour.'

Mia was thoroughly distracted now. She actually smiled at Ellie. 'Me, too.'

She hadn't minded Ellie's gentle touch on the fingers of her uninjured hand as she put her own fingers beneath it to admire the nail polish. She was even more careful as she slipped her fingers beneath those on Mia's injured side.

'Can you move these fingers, darling? I want to see how pink they are.'

Mia shook her head.

'Because it hurts?'

It was a slow nod, this time.

'But it doesn't hurt so much if you keep your arm very still?'

Another nod.

Ellie nodded. And then she raised her eyebrows. 'Did you know...that if a little girl has broken her arm...when the doctors and nurses fix it, she can choose a pink cast to wear for weeks and weeks?' Then Ellie shook her head. 'But I guess you might choose a green one.'

'*Nooo*... I want *pink*...'

Ellie put her thoughtful face on. 'Hmm...but you'd have to get out of the car and come to where they make the pink casts.'

Mia's face crumpled.

'Tell you what...' Ellie was looking around the car. 'Is that your jacket? The pink one?'

Mia nodded.

'If I put it very carefully behind you, I could tie the

sleeves over the front and that would keep your arm very, very still while we get you out of the car. And if Dr Luke lifts you, you won't have to move at all and it won't hurt more than a little bit.'

Mia started to shake her head but then paused for long enough for Ellie to smile at her again.

'He'll take you to the pink cast place,' she whispered, as if it were a secret.

Mia was still hesitating but Ellie knew they were running out of time. 'What say I make the jacket bandage? And, when that makes you feel better, you can tell us when you're ready to come out of the car.'

She didn't give her time to think about it, already threading one sleeve of the jacket behind the little girl's back and then pulling the puffy fabric through. She kept one sleeve at waist level and pulled the other one up to drape over the shoulder on the uninjured side. And then she made sure there was as much padding as possible around the elbow and pulled the sleeves tightly together and tied them in a firm knot. The injured arm was completely immobile and Mia had done nothing more than whimper a little bit.

It was only then that Ellie straightened, to find Mia's mother and Luke had stopped talking and had been watching her—maybe for all of the few minutes it had taken to get Mia ready to be moved.

She stepped closer to Luke and turned her head so that she could speak very quietly, right beside his ear.

'Looks like a fracture dislocation of her left elbow,' she murmured. 'Limb baselines are well down. No movement in her hand and it feels cold. I don't like the colour, either.'

His gaze met hers. A brief eye contact but, like the

moment they'd both heard the child scream, she knew they were both thinking exactly the same thing. This injury needed to be sorted urgently or Mia might end up with reduced function in her hand. This wasn't the place to try and put in an IV and administer pain relieving drugs. It could be done far more efficiently and safely once she was in the emergency department.

It was Luke's turn to crouch beside the car.

He had to get this child out no matter how much she resisted but, if she struggled, it could well make her injury worse. A broken shard of bone could sever a nerve or a major blood vessel.

He had watched the way Mia had calmed a terrified little girl with a skill that had taken his breath away. Had made something in his gut feel all soft and told him that she was going to be the best mother that Jamie could ever wish for.

All he needed to do now was to follow her example.

'I need you to pretend to be a caterpillar,' he told Mia. 'And you're inside your cocoon getting ready to be a butterfly so you can't move your legs or your arms. Can you do that, sweetheart?'

Big, brown eyes flicked upwards. Was she looking for her mother? Or Mia?

'I'm here, darling,' her mother said. 'I'll be right beside you.'

'You're a pink caterpillar,' Ellie said softly. 'And you're bee-*yoo*-tiful.'

Luke used the distraction to slip one arm behind Mia and the other beneath her knees. On the middle sylla-ble of Ellie's elongated word, he lifted Mia and stepped backwards in a smooth movement but the little girl still screamed in fright.

Luke held her close, careful to avoid any contact with the injured elbow. The splint Ellie had fashioned from the puffer jacket was remarkably good and the elbow was supported as well as it could have been with the kind of inflatable splints or other gear the ambulance service might have used. Having never worked with Ellie, he had been blown away, not only by her skill in winning the trust of a young patient, but her confidence in making an initial diagnosis and initiating the first level of treatment.

To say he had been impressed was an understatement...

Luke was confident that moving Mia hadn't significantly increased her pain level and, sure enough, the child relaxed into his firm hold and became quiet.

'Follow me,' he told the mother. 'I know the quick way into ED.'

Walking past his own car, he noted the open door beside Jamie and glanced over his shoulder at Ellie.

'I'll come too,' she said. 'I'll just get Jamie and the extra car seat and blanket.'

Knowing that Ellie would be following made it feel curiously different, heading into the hospital through the staff only door that gave rapid access to the interior of the emergency department, bypassing the waiting room and triage desks. He almost waited at the door, knowing that Ellie wouldn't have her staff swipe card she would need to open it with her, but the sense of urgency overrode the urge. This little girl had, unexpectedly, become his patient and she was his priority.

No...not just his patient.

His and Ellie's.

And that just made it all the more important to make sure Mia got the best treatment possible.

He'd only been working in this department for a little over a month but Luke was very proud of the response he got, walking in with this injured child in his arms. The treatment was all he could have wished for. A nurse applied an anaesthetic patch to Mia's arm within seconds of him putting her gently down on a bed and a fellow consultant was able to insert an IV line with minimal distress a few minutes later. X-rays were taken and an orthopaedic consultant arrived as the images became available on the computer screen.

Ellie had been correct in her diagnosis. The elbow was both fractured and displaced and the blood and nerve supply to Mia's hand was severely compromised. Thanks to the IV line, enough sedation was easily administered to make the process of relocating the joint and stabilising the fracture swift and completely satisfactory. And Ellie was there, with Jamie in her arms, as Mia blinked sleepily at the bright pink cast that covered her whole arm, keeping her elbow in the bent position it needed to heal.

'Oh...' Ellie pretended to shade her eyes from a blinding light. 'That is *so* pink. I love it.' She touched Mia's forehead, smoothing away an errant tress of red hair, as she smiled. 'Do you feel better now, hon?'

Mia's smile was all the response needed. Her mother was smiling, too.

'I can't thank you enough,' she said. 'I don't know what I would have done if you two hadn't found me.'

'It was our pleasure,' Luke said. 'Wasn't it, Ellie?'

'Sure was.'

Ellie's smile lit up her face and Luke's heart gave a curious little extra thump. He'd suspected that she was missing her job and now he realised not only how much she loved it but how good at it she was.

He could imagine what it would be like to work with her properly. To be on a difficult shift here and know that he had someone like Ellie by his side. Someone he could rely on absolutely. A second pair of hands that belonged to someone who seemed to think along exactly the same lines he did.

She wouldn't be a vulnerable young mother, would she? She would be a trusted colleague.

An equal.

How easy would it be to dismiss an attraction that seemed to be getting stronger with everything Ellie did stirring up feelings of admiration? Pride, even.

No. Luke turned away from that smile to say goodbye to Mia and her mother. It wouldn't make any difference because he wouldn't have allowed himself to act on that attraction. He wasn't even going to be in the country in a couple of months and, in the same way he knew how much Ellie loved her work as an emergency department nurse, he also instinctively knew that she wasn't the type to embark on a relationship that wasn't going anywhere.

The hints of the passion she had displayed to protect her child and keep her independence told him that Ellie Thomas was the type of woman who would fall in love and be just as passionate about being a loving and loyal partner.

The guy that won that love would be the luckiest man on earth. The image of Ellie standing there with her baby in her arms was still in his head even though she was behind him. That unknown man would not only win the love of an extraordinary woman but he would get the bonus of a beautiful baby son.

He'd better love him, Luke thought fiercely. As if he were his own. And he'd better know exactly how lucky he was and protect both Jamie and Ellie as if his own life depended on it.

He would…

In some ways, it was a damn shame he couldn't be that man but that was how it was.

And, with that reminder, Luke felt a surge of relief that that foundation stone had somehow miraculously put itself back together after the alarming moment in the Baby Supermarket.

He knew exactly what he wanted from life and a family had never been in the plan.

And never would be.

CHAPTER SIX

'THIS IS MORE like afternoon tea than lunch. You must be starving.'

'I kind of forget about eating when I'm busy. It's been quite a day so far, hasn't it? Oh, wow…that looks amazing.'

Ellie felt quietly pleased with herself. The last stop on the way home had been a quick dash through a supermarket and she'd put this lunch together. Mini baguettes stuffed with fresh slices of tomato, mozzarella cheese and basil leaves, drizzled with olive oil. She was having a tall glass of sparkling mineral water with a slice of lime but Luke had chosen an icy Mexican lager and had stuffed a wedge of lime down the neck of the bottle.

'It's my day off,' he'd said, leaning past where Ellie was busy at the kitchen bench putting lunch together to open the fridge. 'I reckon I've earned a reward.'

Even without a celebratory drink, this was a reward for Ellie, too.

They were sitting outside the kitchen on the overgrown terrace. The table beneath the canopy of a rampant grapevine was shaded from the surprising warmth of the autumn sunshine and Jamie was also in the shade, asleep inside the mountain buggy pushchair that went flat enough to be a pram as well.

For a long while, they ate in silence.

Nothing had ever tasted quite so delicious and Ellie couldn't think of anyone she would rather be sharing this food with.

Covert glances became more frequent. There was something profoundly satisfying watching a man taking such obvious enjoyment from food you had prepared. She loved the way Luke closed his eyes as he savoured his first mouthful and the way he wiped his mouth with the ball of his thumb to remove an errant crumb or drops of moisture the neck of his beer bottle had left behind.

When Luke had reached behind her to get at the fridge, his arm had brushed close enough to her back to give her a shiver that felt as if it could turn into goose bumps. Every glance she allowed herself now could bring back that little shiver that started somewhere in her spine and then sent tiny forks of lightning deep into her belly.

And they were as delicious as their meal and this perfectly peaceful, idyllic setting. The silence didn't feel at all awkward. It felt completely comfortable—as if she and Luke knew each other well enough to simply relax in each other's company.

It wasn't exactly silent at all, Ellie realised, then. She could hear the hum of bees amongst the wash of lavender flowers that were so thick and heavy, the old hedge was obscuring the stone path leading away from this courtyard. And the birds on the edges of the forest nearby... It was a long time since Ellie had heard the distinctive call and clicks of the native tui. She recognised the cheerful background song of wax eyes, and she would have known the squeak of her favourites—fantails—even if she hadn't noticed them sharing the insect life with the wax eyes amongst the bunches of grapes weighing down the vines above them.

'Do the fantails come into the house?' she asked. 'They used to do that all the time when I was a kid.'

'I haven't noticed.' Luke took a swig of his beer and gave Ellie another shiver as he brushed his lower lip with his thumb. 'But you're right. I remember them doing that, too.'

'My mother told me that there's a Maori myth that they're messengers from the spirit world and they bring death or news of death.' Ellie shook her head. 'I never believed it. They're such happy, friendly little birds.'

Luke grinned. 'So you're going to rewrite the myth to give them a positive spin?'

Oh…that smile… It made the day even brighter. And the warmth in those astonishing hazel eyes made this tiny patch of the world even more of a blissful oasis. Ellie knew she was in trouble, here.

Last night, she had been able to dismiss the pull she felt towards this man as a product of emotional overload following a traumatic experience heightened by exhaustion. But she'd had enough sleep to revive her and her immediate future was looking less worrying by the hour. Luke had even told her she didn't have to rush into finding a new place to live.

The thought of spending more time with Luke—like this—was…

A dream come true?

It wasn't just the remnants of a teenaged crush. Or that she had felt as if she was coming home in returning to Kauri Valley. Okay, both those things had probably contributed and sped the process up but there was something much bigger than that going on, here.

In that split second of holding Luke's gaze as she basked in that smile, Ellie felt something so astonishing it took her breath away.

Something that felt like a combination of liquid and light. As if it could trickle into all the gaps and cracks in her life—and her heart—and light up the fact that they had been made whole.

Oh, boy…she really was in trouble. This was way more than physical attraction. And if Luke guessed even a fraction of what was going on in her head and heart, he would think she was completely crazy and run for the hills.

Amazing how such a revelation could happen in the blink of an eye but Ellie knew she'd held his gaze long enough to give it significance, so she shrugged as she looked away, to make the eye contact as unimportant as her dismissal of a sombre myth.

'Why not? Enough bad things happen in life without looking for signs of them before they arrive.'

'True. We're both used to seeing what life can throw at people. They get carried through the doors of emergency departments every day.'

Ellie nodded. 'I had a good catch up with Sue while you were helping to sort Mia's elbow. She told me about that baby with whooping cough last night.'

Luke stopped eating. His eyes widened with what looked like dismay. 'Oh, man… I should have told you about that myself.'

'Sue said it was you who thought of it—that it wouldn't have occurred to her to worry about whether

I'd had a booster or not. I have, by the way. And he's only two weeks away from getting his own vaccination.'

'And I had a booster when I was doing that obstetric stint. Just to be on the safe side.'

Satisfied, Luke turned his attention back to his meal but Ellie's attention had drifted.

It had given her an odd frisson, knowing that Luke had been thinking of her without any prompting. Sue had been just as surprised. And then her friend had been completely blown away by the knowledge that Ellie was staying with Luke.

'*He's gorgeous,*' she had whispered, keeping her voice down even though they were alone in the staff room. '*I certainly wouldn't have said no to an invitation like that.*'

'*We're just friends,*' Ellie had whispered back. '*But you should see his house. It's actually got a turret. Like something out of a fairy tale.*'

'*Wow... I'd love to see it. Can I come and visit?*'

'*Don't see why not. Some time when Luke's at work, maybe. Text me.*'

It wasn't the only thing about this situation that felt like magic. Luke had come to rescue her like the impossibly handsome hero of the story. A prince, even, seeing as his house had a turret like a tiny castle. She had been showered with gifts. And now they were having a small feast in the most romantic of settings. What would happen next? Would Luke push his plate away and take hold of her hands and declare his undying love?

Things like that did happen in fairy tales, didn't they? Love at first sight that everyone knew would last for a lifetime...

Oh, boy...it was high time Ellie got back in touch

with reality. Her gaze drifted to the path obscured by
the neglected lavender hedge.

'Where does that path go?'

'Through Mum's rose garden and down to the vegetable garden and then into the orchard. Or what was
the vegetable garden. Judging by the state of the rest of
the garden, I expect it's disappeared.'

'We had a veggie garden.' This was good. Normal,
friendly conversation. Ellie could try and cover up the
lingering shockwaves of that revelation. For her own
sake more than Luke's, in fact. He wouldn't need to run
for the hills, would he? He wasn't even going to be here
for more than another couple of months. However huge
this discovery felt, nothing was going to come from it.

'It used to be a chore to have to go and pick all the
beans or peas for dinner.' Did Luke notice that her
cheerful tone was a little forced? 'Or dig up some carrots or potatoes but when I look back, it was an amaz-
ingly healthy diet.'

'Mmm.' Luke was reaching for another bread roll
seemingly as relaxed as he had been. Thank goodness
telepathy didn't actually happen. 'I still have fond memories of the food Mum used to make. Wonderful cas-
seroles that had been in the oven for hours and baked
potatoes with crispy skins. I'd get home from school on
a cold winter's day and the smell would hit me as soon
as I walked through the door.' His smile was poignant.
'It smelt like home...'

Jamie stirred and whimpered—an oddly appropriate
response to the note of sadness in Luke's voice. Ellie
got up to take hold of the pushchair's handles so she
could move it gently back and forth.

Her heart was being squeezed painfully from that

note in his voice. This place was still his home but either he didn't realise that or he had no intention of staying here because it was too difficult for some reason. Because it meant too much? In either case, he was going to run away from it. To some huge city like London or Boston where it would take hours to fight your way through traffic and find a bit of countryside or a beach that would remind him of home.

How sad was that?

Ellie suppressed a sigh. 'I wonder how many kids get to eat food from their own gardens like that these days.'

'They probably still do around here.'

Ellie tossed a smile over her shoulder. 'It was a great place to grow up, wasn't it? Do you remember sliding down those huge sand dunes at the beach?'

'Using rubbish bags as toboggans?' The glint of remembered pleasure lit up Luke's face. 'Yeah... Surfing was even more exciting, though.'

'We never surfed. But we had a friend with a pony. She used to let us have a go down on the beach. I galloped once...bareback. Now, that was exciting...'

We. It was still automatic to include Ava in those childhood and adolescent memories. It was Ellie's turn to feel the sad whisper of loss. Maybe it wasn't so incomprehensible that Luke would want to put as much distance as possible between his current life and his childhood memories.

She searched for something positive to chase away the negative pull. What had started this trip down memory lane, anyway?

That was right...food...

'I'm going to try and find a place to rent that has

enough space for a veggie garden,' she declared. 'I'd like Jamie's first food to be stuff that I've grown myself.'

'Sounds like a great idea. A house instead of an apartment, maybe.'

Ellie shook her head. 'Houses are out of my price range.'

The wheels of the pushchair caught on a particularly large weed growing in the crack between two big stones. She stooped and pulled at it, surprised to find how easily it came up. It seemed as if the stones had sand between them rather than soil. She pulled at another one and it slid out with a satisfyingly long set of roots still intact.

'Are you okay for money?' Luke asked quietly.

Ellie bristled. He'd already provided far too much and tried to wave off her offer of repayment. What was it he'd said?

Oh, yeah...

That he had no dependants and didn't intend to 'get saddled' with any...

She'd been right this morning, hadn't she, when she'd interpreted that look on his face as advertising that a family of his own would be his worst nightmare?

This oasis of peaceful countryside on a sunny afternoon suddenly seemed a lot less blissful with that cold shower of reality doing a good job of extinguishing the glow of any powerful emotions Ellie had been experiencing.

Jamie had settled again so there was no need to keep rocking the pushchair. Ellie took another step away from where Luke was still enjoying his late lunch and swooped on another patch of weeds. There was something almost soothing in ripping up these invaders and tossing them aside.

'I'll be fine,' she muttered, finally, in response to Luke's query about her finances. No way was she going to confess how tough things were. She'd had a big student loan to pay off and she hadn't hesitated to help out during the years of her mother's terminal illness.

She summoned a confident tone. 'I'm thinking that Jamie will be old enough to go in child care by the time he's three months old and that's only eight weeks or so away.'

Really? The last few weeks had gone so fast. How hard would it be to hand over the care of this precious baby to people she didn't even know?

Ellie pulled at more weeds, trying to focus on them as she blinked back the threat of tears.

'Wow...' The admiration in Luke's voice broke the new silence. 'Look at what you've done. I'd forgotten what this area even looked like.'

Ellie straightened. She had cleared a surprisingly big patch of the stone paving. And it did look great. The stone had the same grey-blue tinge of the kitchen's slate floor. If it was all cleared and swept, with the French doors wide open as they were now, it would make an almost seamless extension of the house into the garden. Indoor, outdoor flow. That was something real estate agents got excited about.

'I'll finish it,' she said. 'And I can trim that lavender hedge, too, if you've got some tools.'

'You don't have to do that. I'm going to find a landscaping firm to come in.'

'You said they were expensive. And hard to find.' Ellie looked up at the grape vine, which would need heavy pruning soon, and then at the tangle of rose bushes behind the lavender hedge. She thought about the neglected vegetable garden that she hadn't seen yet. And then she grinned at Luke.

'I could do it,' she said.

'Do what?'

'Sort your garden out. As thanks for letting me stay.'

Luke shook his head. 'It's too big a job. And you've got more important things to do—like finding a new place to live.'

But he'd said there was no rush about that. If she was doing a good job with the garden, maybe he'd be happy for her to be around a bit longer, even.

'I'd enjoy it. I'll be doing most of my flat-hunting on-line, anyway, and I'd love the chance to be doing something outside when Jamie's asleep. I've been living in a bedsit for so long. Being here...' Ellie stretched out her arms to encompass the rambling, old house and the courtyard and gardens beyond. 'This makes it seem like it was even more of a prison than it felt like sometimes.'

The idea was brilliant. She would love the challenge and the physical exercise would help her get her body back into shape. It was just a bonus that it would be a reason to stay near Luke a bit longer.

Wasn't it?

But Luke was still looking more than a little doubt-ful. Ellie stepped towards him.

'Please?' Suddenly this was very, very important. She didn't want to leave this place.

Not yet, anyway.

She summoned what she hoped was her best, winning smile, catching her bottom lip between her teeth when it felt a bit too much.

'You've done so much to help me. I'd really like to be able to do something for you...'

CHAPTER SEVEN

No man alive could have resisted that smile.

Not with that kicker of vulnerability that biting her lip like that advertised.

It wasn't relief that Luke was feeling.

Okay, it *was* relief but it wasn't due to the realisation that Ellie wasn't going to disappear out of his life just yet. It was because she'd have enough time to find a perfect place to go to and then he could stop worrying about both her future and Jamie's. Expecting her to disappear in a few days was ridiculous.

She not only had to find new accommodation but probably furnish it as well.

She also had to sort out her transport issues by collecting that rental car and had she not realised how short of clothes she was? She was still wearing the same tee shirt she'd had on last night when he'd rescued them and, right now, it was getting rapidly filthier. His, albeit reluctant, agreement to her plan had apparently triggered a level of excitement that had her exploring more of the garden—pulling up the closest and biggest weeds that came to hand. What had been a largely white tee shirt with a bird and some heart-shaped spots was now streaked with green plant juice and smudges of dirt.

Swallowing the last bite of those delicious rolls Ellie had put together, Luke wiped his mouth and had to shake his head as she pushed her way back through the rampant lavender bushes.

'I'll find you a clean tee shirt,' he offered. 'I've got plenty, as long as you don't mind black.'

Ellie looked down at herself and groaned. 'I didn't even think about that. I'd better put some clothes shopping at the top of the list after I sort out that rental car tomorrow.'

She came closer and peered into the pushchair at Jamie. Her hair had a small, leafy twig caught in it and Luke just couldn't stop himself reaching out. Ellie jumped as he touched her head.

'Keep still. You've got something caught in your hair.'

Ellie kept very, very still as he carefully disentangled it. She also kept her gaze very firmly on her baby so it was weird that this suddenly felt so...intimate?

'There you go.' He held out the twig to show her. 'You might want to wear a hat if you're really going to take on a job as a gardener. And some gloves...' He felt his gut twist as he noticed a scratch on her arm, deep enough to be oozing blood.

How ridiculous was that? He saw people bleeding all the time. Life-threatening amounts of bleeding, come to that, and he never felt anything like this. As if the damage had been done to his own skin.

'I'll add stuff like that to my list.' Ellie nodded briskly and her businesslike tone was exactly what Luke needed to make things feel normal again. And then she lifted her gaze to meet his and her smile made things even better. There was a familiarity there that only came with friendship. The kind of friendship where it was safe to relax because the people involved liked each other.

Trusted each other.

Genuine friendship was the best thing in life as far as Luke was concerned. Something to be valued enormously. Definitely not something to sabotage by letting physical attraction get out of control. To have both at the same time had proved incompatible more than once in his life because those women always wanted more.

Too much.

They wanted long term commitment. Babies...

'I could drop you in to the rental car place tomorrow, if you like. It'll be early, though—I'm switching to day shift for a while.'

'Brilliant. Thanks, Luke. And...um...' The glance she gave him was uncertain.

'What?'

'Well... Jamie looks like he's going to sleep a bit longer and I... I *really* need a shower. I could put him in the bathroom with me, but he might wake up if I move him and...'

Luke waved his hand. He could do this for a friend. 'Go. It's fine. He can stay here while I clear up lunch. It's no problem.'

Jamie wasn't the problem, he decided, as he ferried the plates and glasses back to the kitchen bench. What was a bit of a problem was that he could hear the water running in the bathroom down the hall. And his mind refused to stop picturing Ellie in there.

Naked.

Covered with soap suds.

Friends did not think about each other like that. Or, if they did, it didn't generate a fierce tingle of desire.

This wasn't going to be easy. It might even prove to be the biggest challenge Luke had ever faced.

But maybe that was a good thing? If nothing else, it could override the challenge that walking away from this place for ever was going to present. And he had to walk away because there was nothing here for him any more except ghosts from a past that could stop him embracing the future he had planned.

Jamie woke up and let out a squawk that demanded attention. Luke held the handle of the pushchair and rocked it back and forth, the way he'd seen Ellie doing earlier.

It didn't even occur to him to pick the baby up. Comforting babies was not in his skill set. He was quite happy to deliver them or to examine and treat them when they were sick or injured. He could even tickle their tummies and make them smile occasionally but to pick them up and cuddle them?

No way. He avoided that like the plague.

Okay, he had picked Jamie up once but that had been because it had been too painful for Ellie to move much on that first night. It wasn't as though he'd done it because he wanted to hold a baby himself.

It was just as well he hadn't ever wanted a family of his own, wasn't it?

He didn't actually *like* babies when they weren't presenting an interesting medical challenge.

Even Jamie? Even when he'd experienced that very odd moment of connection in the first minutes of this new life? A connection that had made holding him that first night feel different from any other infant he'd ever touched? He hadn't put him down in a hurry, had he? Even when he'd stopped crying...

Luke joggled the pushchair in addition to its horizontal movement.

Especially Jamie, he decided. That was one boundary he had no intention of being forced to break. And that was a challenge that he knew would be no problem at all to meet.

It wasn't just the change in working hours that made Luke's life so different over the next week.

He'd always chosen to live alone as an adult. Because he liked his own company and the independence of his own space.

For someone that didn't even like babies, this new arrangement should have been unbearable.

It was anything but...

He found himself looking forward to getting home at the end of the day. To grabbing a cold beer from the fridge and heading outside to admire the progress that Ellie was making. The courtyard had been cleared of weeds by the end of the first day. The lavender hedge had been clipped back the day after that and then Ellie had tackled the rose gardens, pruning bushes, pulling out weeds and uncovering an astonishing number of flowering plants that he'd had no idea were even there.

'I wanted to mow the lawns,' she told him. 'But they need something with more grunt than the lawnmower, at least for the first cut.'

'There should be a weed eater in the shed. That was one of my jobs, way back.'

'Yeah... I found that. But it's covered with cobwebs and I couldn't get it started.'

'I'll sort it on my next day off. We'll need some fresh two-stroke. The chainsaw will need that as well.'

Ellie's eyes lit up. 'You can use a chainsaw? That's awesome... There's a lot of branches that are too thick for the pruning shears. And you don't have a rotary hoe, by any chance, do you?'

'Don't think so. Why?'

'The veggie gardens are full of waist high weeds. It's going to be a big job.'

'Hmm... We'll take a look at that when there's more daylight.'

Did he really want to spend one of his precious days off working in a garden that wasn't even going to be his in the near future? It should have irritated the hell out of him.

But, strangely, it did nothing of the sort.

Watching the garden he remembered so well emerge from the neglected wilderness was a poignant kind of magic. His parents had loved this garden. It might have been a chore having to help with weed eating and mowing grass and clipping hedges when he was a teenager but it had been part of the only family life he'd ever had.

Making things good again now felt like paying homage to that part of his own story. The part that had made him the person he was now instead of what...a prison inmate?

Or dead?

Yeah...either of those outcomes had been a real possibility the way his life had been heading before the Gilmores had taken him in.

He'd fully expected that having someone else in his house would have disturbed him a lot more than it did. Maybe it was because it was helpful having someone around most of the time. He'd been able to get people in to mend the windows and those dodgy boards on the veranda and now had painters booked to come and redo the exterior of the house. And maybe it was more than acceptable because Ellie had taken it upon herself to cook dinner every evening.

He had no idea where she got the level of energy she had from. She was a new mother, for heaven's sake. Surely looking after the demands of an infant twenty-four hours a day was enough of a job? But Ellie seemed unstoppable. She had her own transport now and she'd even been out to view a couple of rental properties that had looked promising online—in between sessions in the garden, shopping for food and producing meals that meant Luke walked into a house that smelt as welcoming as this home had been to a starving teenager.

It felt...special.

Part of the paying homage thing?

Not that he was going to try and analyse those moments when something deep tugged at his heartstrings. He told himself that it was simply confirmation that this house needed a family. That he was right in having told Mike the real estate agent that this property was not going to be marketed as anything other than an idyllic family home. In telling his solicitor that he needed to do everything in his power to make sure that the distant cousin, Brian, couldn't make any claim on this land and use it as a development opportunity. Some progress was being made on the contesting of the will issue apparently but Mike was still ringing every other day to try and get the nod to start the marketing process.

'This is a property that needs to be marketed internationally. It takes time to book advertising space. Get a billboard made. Print brochures. At the very least we have to get the photo shoot done. I've got a guy with a drone who can do some spectacular aerial views. You won't even *see* any weeds in the gardens.'

That *had* been irritating. Luke had finally told him that he had to wait until the garden had been sorted before any photographs could be taken. It didn't matter that weeds wouldn't show up in aerial photographs. It was important to him that this place looked its absolute best.

If that meant rolling up his sleeves and getting his hands dirty in the garden himself, then that was fine by him.

Like living here again, it would be a trip down memory lane. An opportunity to be thankful for the twist his life had taken all those years ago. A chance to say goodbye properly before he moved on?

Maybe the most disturbing thing about having Ellie here were the broken nights.

Not because his sleep was interrupted. He'd got more than used to that back in the days of being a junior doctor covering way too many night shifts. The cry of a hungry infant was no worse than a pager going off. A lot better, in fact, because he didn't have to get up. He could just roll over and go back to sleep.

The disturbing part was that he found himself lying there listening for the sound of Ellie's soothing voice. The sudden silence that meant she would be breastfeeding Jamie. It was easy to drift back to sleep then. What he couldn't control were the images of Ellie's breasts that haunted his dreams and meant waking, as often as not, in need of a cold shower to start his day.

But he was coping. Becoming more confident that

he could meet a kind of physical challenge he'd never had to face before.

More than simply coping, in fact.

That it was Ellie Thomas he was sharing this time with was helping. They had shared memories of this area and the school they had both attended. They knew a lot of the same people. They had both stolen lollies from Mr Jenkins, for heaven's sake. And gone sliding down the same sand dunes. She was part of the past but would also be a link in the future when he no longer had a place to call home, here. She would be that link because they were developing that real friendship more convincingly every day and that friendship was making it a lot easier to resist the powerful physical attraction that he was plagued with.

He wanted to keep this friendship.

He wanted to keep in touch and hear about Jamie's milestones like his first tooth and first, wobbly steps. He wanted to see pictures of him blowing out candles on his birthday cakes and maybe a video clip of him jumping in puddles or kicking a ball. A proud smile on the first day of school...

He'd been there to feel the utter relief when this baby had taken his first breath and there would never be another child that he felt such a connection with.

Or another woman, for that matter.

Ellie had cooked a roast chicken for dinner tonight and the smell wafting through the house made Luke's mouth water. He headed straight for the kitchen. The French doors were open and Jamie's pram was positioned to catch the gentle warmth of the last sunbeams of the day. That light was also filtering through the grapevine outside, the dappled shadows shifting over the rustic table and long bench seats on either side, and dancing over the newly swept paving. Big terracotta urns had been freshly scrubbed, he noticed, and planted with bright red flowers. Geraniums?

He hadn't realised he'd spoken aloud until Ellie rewarded him with a quick grin.

'Wow…a man that can name a flower. I'm impressed. I picked them up when I went past the garden centre today. Do you like them?'

'It all looks fantastic out there. You've even started doing things out the front, haven't you? It was a lot easier to walk down the path.'

'I've started. There's some tree branches that will need your skill with the chainsaw when you finally get that day off. I've put them on the list.' The wiggle of Ellie's eyebrows suggested that the list was already quite long. 'You hungry yet?'

'Starving. Didn't have time to stop for lunch.'

'That's not good.' Ellie gave him a stern look. 'You need to build your strength up for your gardening gig.'

He found a beer and watched as Ellie took the chicken out of the oven and put it on a carving dish. Then she scooped crispy looking vegetables out of the roasting pan and put them into a big bowl. It was when she put the pan onto the stove top, clicked the gas flame into life and sprinkled flour into the pan that Luke felt another one of those tugs on his heart that was powerful enough to feel like pain.

Dorothy Gilmore used to do exactly that.

'Real gravy doesn't come out of a packet, son,' she'd say. *'It takes time. And love…'*

He had to step away from the memory. What would Ellie think if she looked up and saw tears in his eyes?

'So what else did you do today?'

'I got some more clothes. Look…*real* jeans…' Ellie left the wooden spoon against the edge of the pan as she held her arms out and did a quick pirouette.

Luke frowned. They looked like perfectly normal jeans as far as he could see. A denim casing for a pair of very nice legs and a particularly shapely bottom.

Ellie had seen his puzzled frown. 'They're not maternity jeans,' she explained. 'They don't have a stretchy insert to fit my enormous belly.' She patted that part of her anatomy. 'Still a bit squishy, I have to say, but it's definitely improving.'

'You've got nothing to worry about. You look amazing.'

The words came out before Luke had time to consider any repercussions. Even if he had given it some thought, he wouldn't have expected the startled look in Ellie's eyes. Or the way time seemed to stop even as a flush of colour crept into her cheeks.

It was Ellie who broke that eye contact. So quickly he might have been able to convince himself that he hadn't seen what he thought he'd seen.

Except that wouldn't work, would it, because he recognised the intensity in that fleeting glance and he knew, beyond a shadow of doubt, that Ellie was experiencing the same level of physical attraction to him that he was grappling with in the other direction.

He was in trouble, here.

As if things hadn't been difficult enough when he thought that the attraction was one-sided.

Ellie was stirring gravy as if her life depended on making sure there were no lumps in it.

'Want to eat outside? It's not too cold yet.'

'Sure. I'll grab some plates.'

Outside would be good. Closing the doors might ramp up the sudden tension that seemed to be in the air.

What else could he do to try and defuse it?

Luke cleared his throat as Ellie put down the last platter of food on the table outside.

'Did you go and see that place in Takapuna you were telling me about last night?'

'Yeah...'

'No good?'

'No.' Ellie's sigh was heartfelt. 'The pictures didn't show that it was right on a main road and that the back garden was a junk yard. I actually *saw* a rat.'

'Good grief...'

'Not to worry. There are new places going up every day. I'll find something.'

She would. But as Luke closed his eyes in appreciation of that first mouthful of moist chicken smothered in gravy, a sudden thought flashed in completely from left field.

What about *this* place?

He could let her live here and care for it. It wasn't as if he had to sell the place to survive financially. He didn't even need the rent and the property would only continue to grow in value, which would make it a fantastic investment.

Jamie would be safe. And he would grow up having the kind of childhood that Luke had never had, right from the start.

But...

Even the perfect crunch of the potatoes that gave way to their smooth soft centres wasn't enough to slow the out-of-control speed of Luke's train of thought. It was inevitable that they were going to crash.

If he did that, he'd be tied. He would have a woman and child depending on him.

He would be responsible for the safety and happiness of others.

As if he had his own family...

'I had a call from my solicitor today.' He had told Ellie about the problem Brian Gilmore had presented. 'The will's been upheld and can't be contested. I'm free to put the place on the market as soon as I'm ready.'

'Oh...' Ellie seemed to be concentrating on cutting the food on her plate into very small pieces. She often did that, he'd noticed, in case she ended up having to feed Jamie and eat one-handedly. She didn't even look up when she spoke.

'Just as well we're getting the garden in shape, then. Not that it would make a difference. I'll bet the first person through will buy it.'

'It has to be the right person.' Luke was focusing on his plate now, too. Weird that one of his favourite meals wasn't tasting as good any more. 'A family.'

Or at least the promise of a family. Like a couple and their new born baby.

Like him and Ellie and Jamie?

Luke's fork clattered as he dropped it onto his plate.

'I'm going to get another beer. Do you want anything?'

Ellie shook her head. Her smile looked forced.

'No. I'm good.'

Luke pulled his phone from his pocket as he stood in front of the fridge. He pulled up Mike the real estate agent's number and tapped in a message.

Had the all-clear to put the property on the market. Drop over later this evening if you want to get the agency agreement signed.

He stared at the screen for a long, long moment. And then he hit 'send'.

CHAPTER EIGHT

IT HAD ONLY taken as long as a single heartbeat but something huge had changed.

One glance…

Had Luke actually meant to give her that compliment on what he thought of her body shape?

Maybe not. Maybe he'd surprised himself and that was why, for that instant in time, he had dropped his guard and Ellie could see the blaze of desire in his eyes.

And, oh, my…she had felt it ignite an apparently endless supply of tinder-dry fuel in her own belly, the heat flooding her entire body. Even her face had probably ended up looking as if it would be possible to fry an egg on her cheeks.

Luke must have seen—and worse, understood— exactly what her response had been.

She'd thought initially that he would be horrified to know how attracted she was to him because he wouldn't be remotely interested in her in the same way. Now she knew that he was and yet he seemed to be just as appalled.

He'd put up what felt like an impenetrable barrier.

Starting the process of putting the house on the market had been the first sign of the distance being created.

A reminder that being together in the same house was a temporary situation.

On his day off, Luke had been more than willing to dust off the old tools in the garden shed and do whatever Ellie had asked. He'd cheerfully pruned back the larger branches that needed a chainsaw and spent hours attacking long grass, first with the weed-eater and then with the lawnmower. Ellie could only watch from a distance, often with Jamie in her arms, and wonder if he'd been this happy to spend his day working outside because it meant that he didn't need to be anywhere near her and conversation, for most of the day, was impossible due to the noise he was generating.

The sensation of a clock ticking to make sure she didn't forget how temporary this was increased when the team of painters arrived and put up scaffolding to work on the outside of the house. Visible changes were happening day by day as one week blended into the next.

Hidden changes were also happening as that barrier became thicker. Even eye contact seemed fraught now and best avoided. There was an elephant in the room that only seemed to be getting larger as they both avoided it so carefully. On the day that Ellie had her six-week postpartum check-up and the doctor told her cheerfully that she was fine to resume her normal sex-life, just being in the same room as Luke was enough to make her blush. She didn't dare risk eye contact. It was almost a blessing that Jamie was more grizzly than usual after his first vaccinations so he kept her fully occupied and, when he was finally settled, Ellie was too tired to do anything other than fall into bed herself.

Luke's impatience to get on with the rest of his life

became clear as he spent evenings working on applications for new positions and sent them off to London and Boston. He even found one in Washington DC that piqued his interest.

Sue came out to visit one afternoon that week and, while she was watching Ellie change Jamie's nappy, she told her friend that everybody knew that Luke had also been offered a permanent position at North Shore General hospital.

'Everybody's hoping he's going to accept the offer. He's fabulous to work with.'

Ellie's heart had skipped a beat. That would mean that—in the not too distant future—she and Luke would be working together.

But then she'd shaken her head.

'He's applying for jobs that have way more to offer. Why would he choose to live here and not in London or New York?'

'Yeah…' Sue's sigh sounded envious. 'I'd be off like a shot, myself. How exciting would that be? He's so good at what he does, too. I would think that he could get any job he wants. Ooh…can I have a cuddle now?'

Ellie helped settle Jamie into Sue's arms. Her smile was automatic but her heart was sinking. Apparently, the job that Luke wanted was somewhere on the other side of the world. Anywhere that was as far away as he could get from her and Jamie?

'Oh…he's gorgeous.' Sue sounded misty as she smiled down at Jamie. 'I want one.'

'No, you don't,' Ellie told her. 'Not until you've got a baby daddy who wants to help, anyway. Being a single mother is…' It was her turn to sigh as she sat down on the couch beside Sue. 'Well…life-changing, that's for sure. Nothing will ever be the same.' She reached out to touch one of the adorable starfish hands Jamie was stretching out into space. 'Not that I'd want to be without this little one. Not now...'

'Uh-oh...' Sue chuckled as Jamie turned his head and nuzzled her chest, opening his mouth to let out a hungry whimper. 'I can't help you there, mate. Here... you'd better go back to Mum.'

She watched as Ellie adjusted her clothing and let Jamie latch on with the same ease and familiarity she'd had in offering her friend a cup of coffee on arrival.

'He's always been good at that.' Sue nodded. 'Do you remember how he got into it when you held him for the very first time?'

Ellie's smile was genuine this time. She would remember for ever just how much her life had changed in those first tugs of a tiny mouth at her breast. Breastfeeding was so much more than simply providing food for her baby, now, and she knew she would make the most of the next few months and cherish this bond that seemed capable of expanding infinitely.

'It doesn't matter how tired you are, or how difficult things have been,' she told Sue. 'When you're feeding them, you can just forget about it for a while and everything in your world is exactly how it should be.'

'Mmm...' Sue's glance was thoughtful. They both knew that Ellie's world was very different than she had intended it to be. 'Have you heard anything from Ava, yet?'

'No. Have you?' Especially in the days before her marriage to Marco, Ava had been very much a part of Ellie's circle of work friends and she and Sue had stayed in touch.

'I don't think anybody has. She hasn't even been on social media since the day Jamie was born. It's been well over a month and she used to update her status every day. It's like she's just vanished.' An angry edge coated Sue's words. 'I can't believe she hasn't at least tried to find out how *you* are.'

'Her life tipped upside down, too. She's got a lot to deal with.'

'And that's the time you need your friends the most.' Sue was frowning. 'What about her family? Do they still live out this way?'

Ellie shrugged. 'I haven't actually been into the village. I've been too busy with Jamie. And helping Luke with the garden here. When I do go out, it's usually to a viewing for an apartment. Or a mad dash through a supermarket.'

Time away from this house and garden felt like an interruption, didn't it? That was something Ellie needed to deal with. However much she loved it, this wasn't her house or her garden. She wouldn't be living here for much longer.

'She'll have to come back at some stage, surely. Will you want to even talk to her?'

'Of course...' Jamie had fallen asleep in her arms, his mouth still on her breast. Ellie eased him upright and began rubbing his back gently. 'We've been friends for ever and I'm worried about her. I want her to know that I'm okay, too. That she actually did me a favour because I know I couldn't have given Jamie away.'

'Maybe you should talk to her mother or something. If there's anybody she would have been in contact with, you'd think it would be her mum.'

Talking to Ava's mother was a good idea, Ellie decided later, but there was someone she would much rather talk to first.

Luke.

And it seemed as if that was a possibility tonight. He hadn't sat down and fired up his laptop as soon as he arrived home from work. He was much later than usual and Ellie had already eaten her own dinner but she had the remains of the casserole and baked potatoes keeping warm in the oven. She knew he would have smelled the hot food as soon as he walked through the door and the pleasure she got from how much he appreciated her cooking for him hadn't worn off. It had become a bit of a joke to ask if he was hungry after the day he'd laughed at her query.

'You create something that smells that good and then ask me if I'm hungry? Silly question...'

But this evening, he simply shook his head in response and, instead, took a beer from the fridge and went outside, to sit down at the table on the terrace.

He was still sitting there, oddly still, when Ellie came back from feeding and changing Jamie and settling him into his bassinet for the night. For a long moment, she stared at the slump of his shoulders through the window.

Something wasn't right.

She poured herself a glass of the red wine she had opened to add to the beef bourguignon that was probably getting rather dry by now but she didn't pause to turn the oven off. She took another glass and the rest of the bottle and walked outside, before she lost her nerve. She tried to ignore the way her heart-rate picked up and seemed to be beating right in her throat.

'Want some company?'

'Sure.'

Ellie poured Luke a glass of wine, too. Asking him how his day had been would be a sillier question than asking if he was hungry when she knew perfectly well something was upsetting him, so she didn't say anything.

She remembered the way he had sat on the end of her bed, the night Jamie had been born, when she had been struggling with the emotional trauma of the surrogacy plan going so terribly wrong. He hadn't tried to encourage her to talk. He'd simply given her the opportunity by sitting there and absorbing her struggle. Offering his company and what had felt like genuine empathy.

That was what she could give him right now. And the empathy was more than just genuine. Looking at hair that was even shaggier than usual after having fingers dragged through it and the deep crinkles around eyes that advertised distress, Ellie had never been more aware of just how much Luke had come to mean to her.

How much she loved this man.

She wanted to reach out and touch the hand that was resting on the table so near her. She wanted to lace her fingers through his and create a physical bond that would let him know that her heart was aching for him. That she would do anything she could to make whatever was hurting feel better.

When the urge became too great, she picked up the small box of matches that lay beside the collection of candles she had impulsively put out here a few days ago but had never bothered lighting because that was a romantic thing to do and that elephant in the room might have got big enough to crush them both.

Now it was just something to do. With a very different kind of tension in the atmosphere, that elephant seemed to have vanished. She took her time, holding the flame of the match to each wick, and she knew that Luke was watching each candle come to life. It took two matches, and it was while she was blowing out the second one that Luke spoke.

'Do you remember that baby with whooping cough that Sue told you about? The one I'd seen the night of your fire?'

Ellie nodded. How could she forget? Inadvertently, maybe, Luke had let her know that he'd been thinking about her and Jamie. That, on some level, he really cared about them and was worried about their welfare. Telling him that Jamie had had his first vaccinations the other day had been one of the most relaxed conversations they'd had ever since that night the elephant had appeared.

'Her name was Grace,' Luke continued. 'She was six weeks old when she came in—not that much older than Jamie would have been, then. And she was pretty sick. The level of cyanosis with each coughing fit had me worried.'

Ellie swallowed hard. It was a parent's worst nightmare to see your baby desperately ill and even hearing the story of a baby she'd never met gave her a clutch of fear for Jamie.

'She got admitted to PICU and kept in isolation for a week. They battled what looked like the start of pneumonia a week or so later but she seemed to be improving. They still kept her in, though, because of an apnoeic episode or two and a low-grade fever that wouldn't go away. I went up to see her on the ward a few days ago.'

Ellie felt the corners of her mouth tilt as she nodded. She'd been surprised when he'd made a follow-up visit when she had been transferred to the maternity ward but it was clearly a normal part of Luke's involvement with his patients and a part of what made him such a good doctor. She was proud of him, she realised. Proud of what he did and what kind of man he was.

'She'd spiked more of a fever and had a bulging fontanelle, which bothered me. And then I heard she'd had a seizure that afternoon and been taken back to Intensive Care. They did a lumbar puncture and an MRI and made the diagnosis of encephalitis.'

'Oh, no...' Ellie whispered. She'd seen babies like that. Sedated and ventilated. Looking so tiny on a bed, with distraught parents hovering nearby. It had been hard enough to see that before she had become a mother herself. Now it was unbearable. She could feel her eyes filling with tears.

'I heard that she died today,' Luke added quietly. 'I can only imagine the agony that those poor parents are going through.'

Ellie didn't say anything. She could do more than imagine it. She could feel the edges of it touching her heart and she had to fight the urge to get up and run to her room to check on Jamie. To touch him. To stand there beside his bassinet and watch him breathing and soak in the awareness of just how precious he was.

'I couldn't do it.' Luke sounded as though he was talking to himself rather than Ellie.

'At least they have each other,' Ellie murmured. If something so terrible happened to her, she would have to face it alone and that was...unthinkable...

She took in a shaky breath. 'Is that why you never want to have kids, Luke?'

She knew she was pushing past a barrier and might

very well be inviting rejection that would hurt but the question came out before she had time to think. Maybe she'd seen a tiny crack in that carefully constructed barrier and the lure of getting a little closer to what lay behind it had been irresistible.

And Luke didn't seem to be pulling away. His body language didn't freeze up. He didn't even reach for his drink. The huff of breath he released suggested surprise more than anything else. As if he hadn't really thought about it enough to put something into words.

'No. I guess it's more like the opposite scenario.'

Ellie frowned. She didn't understand. Luke glanced up in the silence and the darkness of his eyes in the flickering light of the candles made his face look haunted.

'I mean a child left bereft,' he said. 'Rather than the parents. I don't have to imagine how bad that can be because I *know*. I was that child. Left alone and no-body wanted me.'

'Oh… *Luke…*' Nothing could have stopped Ellie touching him now. She wanted to gather that child into her arms and never let him go. He was still there, wasn't he? Somewhere deep inside this amazing man. She couldn't gather Luke into her arms but she could touch his hand. Cover it with her own and give him, at the very least, the human touch of someone who cared.

And Luke accepted the touch. He turned his hand over so that their palms were together and his fingers tightened around Ellie's hand.

'That's something no child should ever have to go through,' she said, softly. She had lost her father when she was young and could remember the enormity of missing him so much but she'd still had her mother and her home—a safe place where she knew she belonged and was loved.

The silence grew. Would Luke say anything more?

Ellie wanted to hear more. She wanted to hear everything.

Finally, he spoke again. Tentatively—as if it was the first time he'd tried out this particular combination of words.

'I was too young to remember or understand, the first time. Well, the second time if you count my mother not even taking me home from the hospital.'

'How old *were* you?'

'Two, according to the records the social services kept. I'd been taken in by a childless couple and then the woman got pregnant, after all. Apparently they didn't want me when they discovered they could have their own children.'

Two years old, Ellie thought with dismay. Just when children were starting to talk and begin to try and understand the world around them.

'The next time I was nearly five and that wasn't really the fault of my foster parents. My foster mum got very sick. She died later but I'd already been moved on by then because the family couldn't cope with looking after me as well as nursing her.'

Ellie could actually hear Luke's painful attempt to swallow. At five years of age, he would remember that abandonment.

He took a deep breath. 'Turned out that was by far the longest time anyone would keep me. I saw the list, once, and there were at least six more foster homes by the time I was ten.' He shrugged. 'I got labelled as a "difficult" child. Nothing worked, apparently—even a good hiding or not being fed. People took me on because they got paid to do it but nobody wanted *me*.'

Ellie could feel the pain in those words and it felt like a physical blow. How big was that button she had pushed when she'd said, out loud—in the first minutes of his life—that nobody wanted Jamie?

Luke must have felt her flinch beneath his hand. The pressure she felt from his fingers was gentle. A crooked smile even appeared on his face as he held her horrified gaze.

'It's okay... I understand completely what made you say that. And I know how much you love Jamie.'

'I'd die for him,' Ellie whispered. 'If it came to that.'

'I hope not.' Luke was still holding her gaze. 'I hope that nothing ever happens to Jamie. Or *you*...'

Ellie found she was holding her breath, waiting for his next words. He looked as though he was about to tell her how much he cared.

That he *loved* her?

'If something *did* happen to you,' he continued very quietly, 'I want you to know that I would do whatever I could to make sure Jamie was okay. And that's a promise. We can get it written up legally so that you'll know he'll always be safe.'

It wasn't quite what Ellie was hoping to hear but it was huge, nonetheless.

'Why?' she asked. 'Why would you do that for Jamie?'

Luke finally looked away. Down at their hands that were still joined. She could see the furrow that appeared on his brow, beneath the shaggy lock that never behaved itself well enough to stay back.

'I'm not sure what it was,' he said. 'But I felt a connection. Maybe it was because of what you said. Or maybe it was because I knew that I was fighting to save his life. I just knew he needed someone in his corner. Someone that was prepared to fight for him.' A tiny shrug rippled down Luke's arm into his fingers. 'I just knew that, in that moment, *I* was that person.'

Ellie's lips trembled. 'Thank you,' she managed. 'Thank you for being there. Thank you for being that person.'

Luke's smile was gentle. 'You're that person now. But I can be… I don't know…an insurance policy?'

Ellie found herself returning the smile without even trying. A slow, soft smile that felt as if it were a neon sign, advertising just how much love she was feeling for Luke.

And maybe it did. Was that why Luke eased his hand away from hers? Why he picked up his glass of wine and drained it? He reached for the bottle and raised his eyebrows in a query. When Ellie shook her head, he refilled his own glass.

'I've never told anybody about the disaster that my childhood was,' he said, then. 'And I'm not going to go horrify you with how much trouble I caused when I got older but it was when I overheard the plan to send me into the equivalent of a prison for teenagers that I ran away. I managed to live rough for nearly a week before the Gilmores caught me.' His smile was wry. 'At least you'll understand now why I'm never going to have a family of my own.'

It was Ellie's turn to frown. 'I'm not sure I do.' He knew exactly how bad it could be when a child didn't feel loved or safe. Surely he was the best person to be able to give them everything they needed. He was prepared to do it for Jamie, who wasn't even his own child, if something terrible happened to her.

'Things can happen,' Luke said, as if he'd overheard her last thought. 'What if I got married and had a kid and I wanted to take my wife away for a romantic weekend, say, and I could because we had hired the best nanny...'

Ellie's eyebrows rose and she smiled encouragingly but her brain had caught on his words and hit a pause button. It wanted to store that idea away, of being Luke's *wife*... Of being whisked away for a romantic weekend...

She had to make an effort to tune in properly again.

'...like a car crash or a plane going down. There's my kid still at home. No grandparents or other family to step in. Just a hired nanny who needs to get back to her own life. What can she do, except to hand over my kid to social services?'

Ellie opened her mouth to say something. To point out that his wife would have a family? But no words emerged. It wasn't a given. *She* didn't have any family. And she didn't want to think about some other woman being Luke's wife.

She wanted to be that woman.

To be with him, every day, for the rest of their lives.

To have moments like this, where he held her hand and talked to her about things that really mattered to him.

To have the support of someone who had already proven how well he could do that. When he'd delivered Jamie. When he'd rescued her after the fire.

When he'd called her *sweetheart*...

So, in the end, she didn't say anything. How could

she hope to change his mind when that would mean, to some level, dismissing how terrible his early life had been?

She couldn't do that. Her heart was still breaking for that small, abandoned boy.

And Luke clearly took her silence as an affirmation of her understanding. She did understand. She might not agree with the rules that had been laid down but, yeah…it was easy to understand.

The elephant in the room had been caged and the reason for its imprisonment was valid. The breath Luke expelled sounded like a sigh of relief.

'Did you ask me if I was hungry a while back?'

She nodded. Found another smile, even, that told Luke she was still his friend. Still grateful for everything he had done for her. Still ready to fight in *his* corner for anything that he needed. And right now, he needed reassurance that she understood. That she could forgive him?

'Yeah… Silly question, huh?'

'You bet. I'm *starving*…'

CHAPTER NINE

MAYBE LUKE HADN'T been aware of how grey and dismal the world had become until the sun had finally edged out from behind a dense layer of clouds.

Ellie knew the truth.

And she understood. She was the only person, apart from Dorothy Gilmore, who had seen the scars that came from being taught that you were unwanted. Unlovable. And, as he'd seen in the eyes of the woman who had chosen to take him on as her son, he'd seen the same acceptance in Ellie's eyes.

The kind of love that came with the bond that only a real family could bestow.

Despite his determination to keep enough of a distance to keep Ellie safe, that was what they'd become over the last few weeks, wasn't it?

A family.

Oh, not the sort that he would have created if he'd chosen to commit to one of those women who'd wanted him to. He hadn't set out to intentionally combine this small group of humanity into a single unit. Fate had stepped in, the way it had when the Gilmores had caught him helping himself to their food, but he could cope with this. He could be an unofficially adopted brother or cousin and offer the kind of support a loving—but separate—family member would provide. An insurance policy for Jamie's future, like the one he fully intended to get his solicitor to put down on paper.

It meant he could channel any feelings he had for Ellie into something very manageable, too. He could admire her and be proud of her.

Love her, in fact. And any sexual attraction could be instantly dismissed as being totally inappropriate. So inappropriate that it seemed as if it had been simply burnt off by the heat of that sun making its appearance from behind dense clouds he hadn't even noticed accumulating.

If he'd needed any proof of that, it had come in the aftermath of that soul-baring conversation about his childhood.

When Ellie had asked him if checking whether or not he was hungry was a silly question. He'd already been feeling as if a weight had been lifted and the mischievous smile she had offered had been...irresistible.

'You bet,' he'd said with a grin that acknowledged the welcome familiarity of what had become a joke between them. 'I'm *starving...*'

Not just for food. For *this*...this...closeness.

The feeling that someone knew more about him than anyone else on earth and could accept his limitations. Could still like him enough to joke with him.

He'd been caught up in that smile. In the first rush of the world seeming so much less complicated. So *right...*?

And yes, maybe it had something to do with the flickering candle light beside them and those gorgeous blue eyes in front of him but it had seemed like the most natural thing in the world to lean closer and kiss Ellie.

Just a soft touch of his lips on hers. An acknowledgement of a new level of friendship. A 'thank you' for being there. For listening and understanding.

And even feeling the astonishing softness of her lips beneath his for that blink of time hadn't unleashed any fierce desire for more than that.

On either side, it seemed. Ellie hadn't even tried to kiss him back. She'd seemed surprised by the gesture but then she'd dropped her gaze and got to her feet with an easy grace that didn't suggest the kiss had been anything more than it had been intended to be—a mark of friendship.

'Let's hope that beef bourguignon hasn't evaporated completely, then,' she'd said lightly.

Being so open with Ellie also meant that Luke could relax.

He could enjoy coming home again—as he had when this had become his family home and he'd had a refuge for the first time in his life.

Everything felt brighter.

Was Jamie aware of the change in atmosphere around him? Was that why Luke had been privileged enough to witness his first smile?

A real smile that made his eyes crinkle and stretched his mouth into a grin that Luke couldn't help returning, just as he hadn't been able to help kissing Ellie the other night.

'What's funny?' Ellie asked, looking up from the pile of laundry she was folding at the kitchen table.

'He's smiling.'

'It's probably wind.'

'No. He's really smiling. Come and see.'

But the new skill wasn't in evidence by the time Ellie came to peer into the pushchair. Jamie just waved chubby fists and kicked his feet to demonstrate his pleasure in seeing his mother.

'Hey...' Luke reached in to tickle his tummy. 'Where's that smile gone, buddy?'

Jamie kicked harder, his gaze now locked on Luke's face. And then, miraculously, he did it again—his lips curling up to make him look like the happiest baby on earth.

'Oh...' Ellie sounded as if she might cry. 'He *is*... he's *really* smiling at you.'

At *him*?

Babies just smiled, didn't they? Surely Jamie didn't recognise Luke as anybody particularly important in his life? He'd never picked him up and cuddled him, or anything.

But it appeared that Jamie did recognise him and that Luke could elicit a smile far more easily than Ellie could in the next few days. He only had to make funny noises or tickle him with just one finger. Weirdly, it made this tiny human seem much more like a real person. Someone he could feel close to. Proud of—as he did of Ellie.

Those smiles were something he could take genuine pleasure in now that he felt more relaxed. Just like the pleasure he was getting in how the house had come to life again, thanks to all the work that Ellie and a small army of tradesmen had done. Damaged boards and windows had been repaired and the new paintwork looked stunning. The gardens at both the front and back of the house were a blaze of colour with the second blooming of so many roses and with the gaps that had been created by her relentless efforts of weeding and pruning now filled with new plants. The photo shoot for the house had been done and Mike the real estate agent's smile had been contagious.

'Stroke of brilliance, putting that bottle of wine and the glasses on that outside table.'

'That was Ellie's idea. She did all the jugs full of roses inside, too.'

'I just wish I'd had time to do the veggie garden,' Ellie said. 'I wanted it to be all cleared with some new rows of baby plants.'

'It didn't show up in the photos.' Mike's smile was encouraging now. 'I'm sure you can have it looking perfect by the time the first viewings happen. Speaking of which…nothing official is out there yet but word of mouth happens in the industry, you know? I've heard about someone who's very, very keen to have a sneak preview and I know they've got the right sort of money to play with. Would you mind if I set up an appointment for next week?'

For a moment, Luke hesitated. Walking away from this house—and Ellie and Jamie—suddenly seemed very, very real. Was that why Ellie seemed to have gone so still? She wasn't looking at him, though. She was looking down at the baby in her arms. Her son. Her future.

One that Luke couldn't continue to be this much a part of.

He glanced back at Mike. 'Sure. Why not?'

Some of the best things in life happened because fate just happened to line up a meeting of the right people at the right time. Luke Gilmore knew that better than anyone.

Ellie's quick glance had a note of something less than happy but Luke chose to interpret it in relation to the last thing she'd said. 'I've got a day off, tomorrow. How 'bout I dig out that veggie garden?'

'It's a big job.'

'Be a good workout, then.'

'Excellent.' Mike left the advance copies of the brochures he had brought to show them and took his leave. 'I'll be in touch...'

It was really going to happen.

Someone was coming to look at the property in a matter of days and, of course, they were going to fall in love with it and offer Luke a ridiculous amount of money that he would be an idiot not to accept.

He would make a final choice from all the amazing job offers he now had to consider and sort out all the loose ends of his past life in New Zealand while he worked the final few weeks of his locum position at North Shore General.

There would be no reason for Ellie to devote all her spare time and energy to this gorgeous old house and garden so she would be able to do what she probably should have already done by now and find herself and Jamie a new place to call home.

As she tucked Jamie into his bassinet for his afternoon nap, she tried very hard to feel positive about it.

'We'll be okay,' she murmured to the sleeping baby. 'We'll find a nice place to live. Make new friends. Mummy will go back to work and you'll love being in day care with all the other babies...'

Oh, dear… The way her words got caught on the lump forming in her throat wasn't a good sign.

She hated the very idea of it, didn't she?

Every bit of it.

Finding a new place to live that had nothing to do with Luke Gilmore. Going back to work quite this soon and leaving her baby in the care of strangers.

Missing Luke with every minute of every day and worse—every night…

Unconsciously, Ellie had put her fingertips to her lips. The way she often found herself doing when she thought back to that kiss.

Just a friendly kiss. The sort you might give to a very good friend to thank them for something important. Like them being okay with knowing that they were never going to be anything more than a friend because they understood exactly why you felt like that.

Trouble was, Ellie was only pretending to understand.

She was in love with Luke.

She still wanted to be with him. So much that it ached right down to her bones when she remembered that kiss because, even though the touch had been so light and so fleeting, every cell in her body had recognised that it was the first note of a song that would be a sound they had been waiting their entire existence to hear and feel.

And, yes, it was stupid to want to go there because it would only make it harder when Luke left but that didn't seem to matter right now. Would it really make a difference when things were already going to be so hard? Ellie was already having trouble imagining her life with Luke no longer in it. It was almost as hard to get her head around as the idea of Jamie not being in her life now.

With a sigh, Ellie turned away from the bassinet, checking that the old-fashioned roller blind was pulled down far enough on the window to prevent any sun shining directly onto Jamie in the next hour or so. It wasn't, so she moved to draw it further down. She would change those blinds if she owned this house, she thought, as she walked towards the window. She'd hang curtains in a romantic fabric, maybe with a flower print, to frame the tall sash windows in soft folds. No flowers if it was Jamie's room, of course, but bright colours. Gold, perhaps, so that it looked like sunshine even in the middle of winter...

Her room was on a corner of the house and this window gave her a view past the edge of the gardens around the kitchen terrace. She could see Luke working in the veggie garden, hauling out the last of the tallest weeds by hand with the garden fork and a spade jammed into the earth nearby, ready for when they were needed for stubborn roots. He'd been out there working for hours already today, with only a short break for lunch, and he had cleared and turned over the earth of more than half of the large patch of land.

It was clearly harder going now, in the burst of autumn afternoon warmth. She saw him pause to wipe sweat off his face with the hem of his tee shirt and she could see the way he pushed damp strands of hair back from his face. It made her smile because she knew how tousled and disreputable it would make him look—as he did sometimes first thing in the morning before he'd brushed his hair.

Ellie loved that look best of all.

She'd take him a cold drink, she decided, picking up the handset of the baby monitor that would let her know the instant Jamie woke up. She might even get an hour or so to help dig before that happened, which was when she was planning to take Jamie for a ride in the car to the garden centre to buy trays of vegetable plants to fill in the newly bare stretch of soil.

The cold glass of water was apparently exactly what Luke had been hanging out for but it seemed to make him feel even hotter. A few minutes later, he stripped off his tee shirt, rolling it up into a ball to mop his face before he continued digging, now wearing only his shorts and a pair of rubber boots.

Ellie was in shorts, too. And a white singlet top beneath a soft, denim shirt. She took the shirt off and hung it over the handle of the wheelbarrow to keep at least one item of clothing clean and then she took the fork and headed for a new clump of weeds, leaving Luke to pull things up by hand and use the spade to turn and chop the soil.

'I'm going to get plants rather than seeds,' Ellie told him, when she carried an armload of rubbish past Luke as she headed for the wheelbarrow. 'That way it'll give people the idea they'll be growing all their own food in no time.'

'Like we did, back in the day.'

'Yeah… I'm thinking broccoli and cauliflowers and cabbage. And beans and peas. Except we'd need frames for them to climb on, wouldn't we?'

'There's a fence buried under the weeds here. I seem to remember that was for beans. With a bit of luck, the posts won't be too rotten.'

'What else did you grow? Potatoes?'

'Of course. Not that you can get them as plants but I remember how to mound up the rows and people will know what they're for.' It was nice that Luke could feel enthusiastic about a garden when he wouldn't be here to taste its produce. 'Carrots,' he added, with a satisfied nod. 'And silverbeet. That was always here. Huge bunches of it.'

'Maybe there's still some hiding.'

'I doubt anything's lasted under this carpet of weeds.'

But Luke struck gold in the very last corner of the overgrown patch when their efforts had brought them close enough to be working together.

'Don't pull that one out,' Ellie exclaimed. 'That's rhubarb...'

Dropping her fork in her excitement, she stumbled over the rough earth to pull the veil of sticky biddi bid weeds from the huge, dark green leaves beneath. Luke reached in to help her but it didn't stop her singlet from getting covered with the tiny green seed balls. Luke even got some in his hair, which already looked the most dishevelled Ellie had ever seen it look. With those tawny streaks to the shagginess, it reminded her of a lion's mane.

And she loved it...

Just as well there was something else to focus on.

'Oh, wow...' She stood back to admire the plants they had uncovered. 'This is fabulous. It's going to make it look like something is really growing and hasn't just been planted for show.'

Luke bent down to snap off one of the long, red stalks. He bit into it but then screwed up his face as if he'd just sucked on a lemon.

'I don't remember this being so sour.'

'Don't try the leaves,' Ellie warned him. 'They're poisonous. And the stalks really need cooking,' she added. 'In a crumble, maybe. Ava and I used to eat it in the garden, though. We'd sneak out a little bowl of sugar and dip the stalks into it with each bite.'

There were so many memories of that old friendship that snuck up on her but seeing Luke's expression had given this one a peculiar poignancy. Raw rhubarb *was* sour and she and Ava had made faces just like that if they hadn't got enough sugar to stick to the stalks. Then they'd giggled and tasted it again just because it was fun.

Shifting her gaze, as if that would somehow shift her focus away from the memories, Ellie noticed all the green balls sticking to the singlet that had been white not so long ago. She'd need to get changed before she went to the garden centre and she would also need to pick off all the sticky balls before she put this garment in to the wash. She remembered this weed from childhood, too. You had to pull every one of those balls off individually, which was exactly what she started to do.

And then she realised that Luke had gone quiet and she looked up to see that he was watching her hands. Ellie had started on the nearest part of the fabric, which was the scooped neckline. Had she even realised that she was calling attention to a cleavage that was rather more impressive than it had ever been before she'd become a mother?

She could feel the warmth of a blush gaining energy. She needed to say something offhand—maybe about how annoying biddi bids were—and then turn back to her own task of forking through the clumps of soil that Luke had turned over with the spade.

Except, she couldn't move. She could feel something changing in the air around her, as if the oxygen were being sucked out by some invisible force. Luke was standing there, half naked. There were streaks on his tanned skin where the sweat had turned dirt into mud. And there were tiny green balls caught on the sprinkling of hair on his chest. A triangle of tawny, sparse hair that trailed into an arrow at the level of the waistband of his shorts.

Ellie tried to catch her breath.

She tried to make her legs work and take her away from this overwhelming temptation to touch Luke.

Neither of those things happened.

What did happen was that she reached out to gently pull a little green ball from where it was caught, just to one side of a nipple that tightened at the first whisper of touch from her fingers.

And just as instantly, Luke's hand whipped up to catch hold of hers and prevent it moving any further.

He was going to reject her, wasn't he?

Gently, of course. It would only take a look to remind her that this wasn't going to happen. That they were only friends. Gritting her teeth, Ellie lifted her gaze to accept that look, fully prepared to give him one of apology on her part.

But what she saw was something very different.

Desire, pure and simple.

A blazing desire but one that only came a little closer to what was coursing through her own veins.

For a long, long moment, they stared at each other in what felt like total amazement.

And then they moved. Ellie had no idea who moved first. It seemed to happen with the speed of light. One moment they were standing there staring and the next, Luke's mouth was on hers.

There was nothing sweet about this kiss. It had nothing to do with gratitude or friendship.

This was out-of-control need.

Pure passion.

A dance of lips and tongues and hands that slid across sweat-slicked skin. It was everything that Ellie had dreamed of except that it wasn't nearly enough...

And somehow, eventually, they both sank onto the rough earth of the garden beneath their feet. Kneeling together. Ellie had her thumbs hooked into the elastic waistband of Luke's shorts and he had his hands beneath her singlet top. Her bra was already undone and she cried out in ecstasy as she felt his hands cup her breasts.

She could hear an echo of her cry. And then another...

Only it wasn't her making that sound. It had a tinny quality that had nothing to do with passion and everything to do with a small baby waking up from his nap.

Ellie had to close her eyes against the crushing disappointment as she felt the moment slipping away, along with Luke's hands.

It was actually embarrassing to have to ease her hands away from Luke's shorts.

Their gazes snagged and held again for another long moment, but the silent communication this time was nothing like the last.

Maybe they both felt a bit horrified as the realisation of how out of control they'd been kicked in.

'I...um... I'll have to go in,' Ellie managed. She stayed on her knees for a moment longer, reaching awkwardly behind herself to find the clasp of her bra.

Luke got to his feet but he made no sound other than a grunt Ellie couldn't interpret. Maybe he was relieved at the interruption. Maybe he was disappointed. Or maybe he just had stiff muscles from all that physical work in the garden.

He offered Ellie a hand to help her up and she took it but it didn't feel anything like the hand that had been caressing her skin only moments before.

And still, Luke didn't say anything. He opened his mouth as if he wanted to, but then he closed it again, uttering nothing more than another uninterpretable sound as he bent over to pick up the garden fork.

Ellie picked up the baby monitor. She glanced over her shoulder as she went to collect her shirt.

He was turning over earth as if his life depended on making this garden look as perfect as possible.

A foot on the fork. A pile of earth turned over. Smacking it with the prongs of the fork helped it fall apart and look like soil ready to accept new plants. Again and again, Luke went through the motions, ignoring the sweat that trickled between his shoulder blades and down his forehead to reach his eyes and make them sting.

How the hell had *that* happened?

He'd had things perfectly under control. He actually managed to take those old twinges of desire for Ellie and turn them into something far more acceptable—an appreciation of all her amazing qualities.

Who knew that they'd been bubbling away under their cover like a volcano getting ready to erupt and it had only needed the provocation of seeing her fingers pulling at the fabric clinging to her breasts as she pulled off biddi bids to blow everything sky-high?

Okay, it *had* needed more than that. What had been his complete undoing had been to see his own desire reflected in Ellie's eyes. That sizzle in the air between them had completely fried his brain.

And then the astonishing *taste* of her... The sensations the touch of her hands created rippling over and then under his skin... The silky softness of her skin that he wanted to taste as much as touch...

Holy heck...if it hadn't been for Jamie waking up when he did, they would have been making love right here on this newly tilled earth. Without any conscious thought of finding protection. Without consideration that this was a woman who'd given birth not that long ago and might not be anywhere near ready for that kind of raw passion.

The kind of passion that would have had them getting even more sweaty and dirty and...

And he'd better stop even thinking about what that might have been like because it was doing his head in.

Luke smacked another solid forkful of earth and watched it splinter and separate with satisfaction. He didn't even pause before jamming the prongs into the ground again. He kept going, until he heard the sound of Ellie's car starting up and then crunching over the loose surface of the shelled driveway and he realised that she was still sticking to the plan and had gone off to buy the new vegetable plants. He could help get them in to the ground later but for now, he had done enough.

A lot more than he'd intended doing, that was for sure. He should be ashamed of himself.

But, if he was honest, he just wanted to turn back time.

And have Jamie sleep a little longer.

It was safe to go inside now, at least, and, man, did he need a shower.

It might have to be one of those cold ones, again, dammit.

The elephant was back in the room.

Somehow, they managed to get through the rest of the day, pretending that things were back to the way they'd been in recent days but, when Luke was clearing up the kitchen as Ellie settled Jamie for the night, Luke knew that something was going to have to be said to defuse the tension that even the hint of eye contact was generating.

Ellie clearly felt the same way. He had his back to her—his hands in the kitchen sink scrubbing dishes—when she came back into the room but he could sense the determination in the way she was moving. The way she pulled a tea towel from the hook beside the old coal range and then came to stand right beside him.

Close enough that he could imagine that he could actually feel heat radiating from the bare skin of her arms.

'We're both adults, Luke,' she said quietly. 'We like each other, don't we?'

Surprise sent Luke's glance skidding sideways to meet hers. *Like?* Such an insipid word to encompass everything he thought about Ellie. It didn't come anywhere near touching the respect he had for her courage and generosity, his admiration for her determination and energy or his appreciation of the way she looked and moved and spoke…

But he couldn't put any of that into words so he simply nodded, hoping his smile would convey a little more than 'like'.

Ellie picked up a plate and began to dry it, as if this were a perfectly normal kind of conversation to have while a household chore was being attended to. 'And we both know this is never going to be anything more than friendship.'

Some of the tension around him evaporated as Luke murmured his agreement but something struck an odd note. Okay, they both knew why he could never let this be more than friendship but did Ellie feel the same way?

Why?

What was wrong with him that would have excluded him as even a possibility of being a life partner?

Another part of his brain could supply the answer to that. A deeply buried part that he'd never prodded in his adult life.

There was a reason that nobody loved you when you were a kid, it reminded him. *You were unlovable. Unwanted... It's why you never stick around any relationship, isn't it? You have to end it first—before anyone else can do it...*

It took a moment to focus on what Ellie was saying now.

'...doesn't mean we're not allowed to get close. If the rules are understood and accepted, why shouldn't we just make the most of something special?'

Luke's hands slowed. He didn't even lift the plate that was now perfectly clean under those soap suds. Ellie's voice was so quiet now it was almost a whisper.

'Something we might never find again,' she said. 'Either of us...'

Luke swallowed hard. Her words resonated with a

truth he couldn't escape. Of course he was never going to find anything like this again. He'd allowed Ellie closer than anyone else in his life.

He trusted her.

And she was confirming that she would never ask him for anything that he wasn't capable of giving her.

If he didn't accept this offer he would spend the rest of his life wondering what it could be like.

To be *that* close to someone you could trust *this* much...

They both wanted it. Luke could feel the sexual energy crackling around him. Burning his skin. He turned to face her, his hands dripping water as he lifted them. He caught the tea towel dangling from Ellie's hands to dry his hands and, for a moment, they were both holding it.

'Are you sure about this?' he asked softly. '*Really* sure?'

Ellie's gaze held his so he couldn't miss the way her eyes darkened. And he could also catch the way her lips tilted up at the corners as she pulled on the fabric they were still both holding. A slow, steady pressure that was firm enough to draw him closer.

Close enough to trap their hands between their bodies. For Ellie's breasts to touch his chest. Close enough for him to feel her breath on his skin as she spoke.

'I think you get the prize for asking the silly question this time...'

CHAPTER TEN

IT COULDN'T LAST, of course.

But, for a precious few days that Ellie would treasure for the rest of her life, she was inside the perfect bubble.

Living in the most gorgeous place on earth.

The mother of the most beautiful child that had ever been born.

Sharing the bed of the man she now knew to be her soul mate.

The sex was every bit as good as she'd dreamed it would be.

No, that wasn't true.

It was far better than she'd dreamed it could be.

She'd been far more nervous than she'd let on, that first time, when she'd made the first move and persuaded Luke that they could add benefits into their friendship. She knew her body had changed after pregnancy and had to hope it was still attractive enough. It was also quite possible that sex would be less than pleasant after the birth. Painful, even.

How weird was it, to feel the same kind of nerves that she remembered having when she'd lost her virginity?

Yet it was entirely appropriate, as well. Because this

was her first time. Her first time to be with someone she was so totally in love with...

And Luke had been so gentle.

So caring.

So in control of a power that Ellie could sense in every touch. A passion that she desperately wanted to experience but lacked the courage to risk unleashing.

That first time, anyway...

The walls of that bubble had taken on a rainbow hue since then.

She was living a fantasy. Caring for her baby and looking after a house and garden that felt like home. Preparing meals with the extra attention to detail that was a pleasure to do when you were making that effort for someone that you loved. Watching the hands move on the old grandfather clock every time she went past, enjoying the increasing thrill of knowing that there was less and less time to wait until the person she most wanted to see would be coming through that door.

Maybe it was living the fantasy that gave rise to new stretches of imagination. Maybe letting go of the past, by leaving the place that had such a connection to it, would persuade Luke that a new future was possible.

With her...

As much as she adored this place, it wasn't what really mattered. She'd go to London with Luke. Or Boston or New York or Washington or wherever he wanted to go in the world. Home was where the heart was, after all, and her heart would always be with Luke. Jamie loved him too—why else would he smile virtually every time he saw him now?

Not that she said anything, of course. That hadn't been part of the deal and Ellie knew perfectly well that

the walls of this bubble were fragile. However beautiful it was, it was a temporary thing.

Unless Luke wanted to change the rules.

Instinctively, Ellie knew that he was the only one
who could do that. That, if she even hinted that something more was possible, she would break the trust between them and Luke would retreat behind the barrier
he'd spent most of his life creating.

Being in this incredible bubble depended on her not
breaking that trust so all she could do was to show him
glimpses of what that future could be like.

Miraculously, Luke seemed just as disinclined to
break that luminescent wall around them all just yet.

It had been his idea to go out, when the sneak preview house viewing had been arranged on one of his
days off. Maybe he didn't want to be there to see total
strangers assessing his beloved home and putting a price
on it any more than Ellie did.

It had been his idea to take Jamie for a walk through
the forest and go down to the beach.

And he was the one who strapped Jamie's front pack
to his own chest.

'I used to know that track like the back of my hand,'
he said. 'I don't want to be worried about you tripping
over tree roots or something.'

Maybe that was also why he held her hand on that
walk.

Not that Ellie minded being looked after as if she
were fragile and feminine. She was, after all, in the
middle of a real-life fantasy that was reminiscent of a
housewife and mother from many decades ago. A simple life when all that mattered was the welfare of your

family and home. Her mother's generation, perhaps. Or more like her grandmother's?

Nothing like real life these days. Or certainly not hers, anyway.

She really had to do something about finding a new place to live and making arrangements for when she went back to work. Her insurance claim was almost settled so there was no excuse not to be sorting out her life.

Except…she didn't want to.

Not yet.

She wanted to walk through a sun-dappled forest like this, feeling the warmth and strength of Luke's hand curled around hers.

She wanted to step back into childhood for a moment and slide down a steep sand dune and see the laughter in Luke's eyes and how wide his grin was.

She wanted to see him tickle her baby and make him smile and smile and smile.

In moments like this, just for a heartbeat or two, it was easy to pretend that they were a real family. That nothing would tear them apart.

In retrospect, it seemed as if it was during that idyllic time together that afternoon that things started to go wrong.

And yet it had been a sigh of pure pleasure that escaped Ellie as she stood on the amazing stretch of white sand that was Moana Beach, shading her eyes from the afternoon sun as she looked out at the offshore islands.

'I'd forgotten that this was one of my most favourite parts of the world.'

'Beautiful, isn't it?' Luke seemed to be watching the curl of the waves. 'If it was summer, I'd be tempted to dust off my old surfboard.'

You could stay, Ellie wanted to say. *You could live here again and have this beach as part of your backyard for the rest of your life.*

But he didn't want that as part of his future, did he? Luke wanted the fast-paced lifestyle of a high-octane career in a big city and maybe a low-maintenance apartment that wouldn't be a drain on his spare time or an anchor if he wanted to move on.

He wouldn't want to be 'saddled' with a property that needed so much maintenance, any more than he wanted that from 'dependants' like a wife or child.

But looking at him now, with a sleeping baby nestled against his chest, and a poignant smile on his face as he remembered the joy of surfing, made Ellie more sure than ever that he was taking his life in the wrong direction. She knew how much the property meant to him—that it was the only real home he'd known in his life—but he was prepared to let it go so that he could be free.

How could he not see that that freedom would deprive him of the best things that life could offer?

The things that she was sharing with him inside this bubble?

'I'll bring Jamie back,' she said, finally, making an effort to keep her tone light. 'When he's old enough to build a sandcastle and go paddling. I'll tell him about what it was like when we were kids and we came here to swim and have picnics and build driftwood tee pees.'

'Don't forget to take him to the General Store.' Luke grinned. 'Mr Jenkins might have been a grumpy old man, but he made the best ice creams.'

'Oh, yes…in a cone. And you could get them chocolate-dipped.'

'And the ice cream would start melting underneath the chocolate and then drip down your arm.'

Ellie laughed. 'That's right... I'd forgotten about that, too. Messy...'

By tacit consent, they headed home. Mike had probably finished showing the potential buyers around the property some time ago.

'I'm not sure that Mr Jenkins still does chocolate dip ice creams,' Luke said sadly. 'I didn't notice them when I went in for milk that time.'

'What about the pick and mix lollies?'

'Yep. They were still there. But they didn't look the same. They all seemed to be things like sour worms and gummy bears. Couldn't see my favourites.'

'Which were?'

Luke gave the question due consideration. 'Milk bottles,' he decided. 'Or maybe jet planes.'

'I was a pineapple lump girl,' Ellie confessed. 'Good grief... I haven't eaten them for so many years.'

'And I've almost forgotten what a jet plane tastes like. Hey...' Luke stopped so suddenly Ellie bumped into him. 'Let's go and get some.'

The glint of mischief in his eyes that accompanied the cheeky grin took Ellie straight back to the time when Luke Gilmore had been the bad boy of Kauri Valley High School. When Ellie had been invisible...

But she wasn't any more. The warmth in Luke's gaze was purely for her. She was so much more than a 'bus buddy' now.

She was his friend.

No. She was much more than that, too. Whether Luke realised it or not, that was a look that could only be shared between lovers.

It was almost too much to bear.

Ellie shook her head as she smiled. 'You wouldn't...'

Luke laughed. 'I didn't mean steal them. I'm talking about a legitimate purchase, here.' He shrugged. 'It will probably be the last time I ever see Mr Jenkins so it would be... I don't know...a fitting farewell?'

There was something in Luke's gaze that made it feel as if he was offering an apology.

To Mr Jenkins?

Or to her?

Ellie could actually feel the crack appearing in her heart and it hurt. She had to force herself to pull in a breath. To keep smiling.

'Sure,' she managed. 'Why not?'

The house and garden were deserted by the time they got back but Ellie could feel that others had been there.

That something had changed.

It was a relief to buckle Jamie into his car seat for the short drive to the village. To see if things hadn't changed there, as Luke had told her that night when he'd been driving her back to her first visit to Kauri Valley in such a long time.

To outward appearances, it did look just the same, with the war memorial in front of the hall and the old pub and the peeling paint on the sign above Mr Jenkins's shop. 'General Store' was an apt description for the random collection of things sold here that ranged from a selection of fresh fruit and vegetables to garden tools, kitchen equipment and haberdashery.

At first glance, the row of plastic containers in front of the main desk where Mr Jenkins ruled over the cash desk looked exactly the same—full of the bright colours of pure sugar confectionery. The pile of tiny, white paper bags was still there, too, waiting for customers to fill by using the miniature shovels in their own container.

Ellie chose pineapple lumps, of course. Luke looked delighted to find the chewy, white lollies in the shape of tiny milk bottles. It was slightly awkward to fill her little bag as she reached around the obstacle Jamie presented in the front pack but she wasn't in the way of anyone wanting to pay for anything. They were alone at the front counter, in fact, because Mr Jenkins was busy with a woman who seemed to need information about a cleaning product. They both had their backs to Ellie and Luke, who both knew that Mr Jenkins was watching them like a hawk.

Expecting them to steal the lollies?

Ellie's lips twitched as her gaze met Luke's and the smile they shared was their own secret.

A moment when the connection between them had never been quite this powerful.

They put their bags on the counter to wait for the opportunity to pay for them, which wouldn't be long because the woman had made her choice. She turned to follow Mr Jenkins to the counter.

And then she stopped in her tracks.

'Oh, my goodness,' she said. 'Ellie…'

It wasn't the tone of someone delighted to see her. Mrs Collins looked horrified, in fact.

Frightened, almost?

Ellie could feel herself stiffen. She could feel Luke edge closer, as if he could sense her need for protection?

'Luke, this is Mrs Collins… Ava's mother…'

Jill Collins was staring at Luke now. 'Luke Gilmore?' She blinked hard. 'I did hear that you were back.'

'I am. Not for long, though.' He smiled at her. 'I didn't realise the news had spread.'

The flicker in the older woman's face told them both that Luke Gilmore would always be remembered around here and Ellie's heart sank. No wonder he didn't want to stay, when so much of the past could be resurrected by nothing more than the twitch of someone's mouth.

Strangely, her head turned sharply, then, as if she expected someone else to be with them but, finally, Jill Collins's gaze dropped to the baby that Ellie had instinctively wrapped into her arms even though he was perfectly safe cocooned in the padded front pack.

'This is Jamie,' Ellie told her. 'I named him after my dad.'

There was a hint of a smile on Jill's face as she nodded once. People around here would approve of that choice. Ellie's father had been a well-liked resident of Kauri Valley. Even Mr Jenkins gave a grunt that sounded satisfied.

''Bout time we saw a new generation around here,' he muttered. 'Place feels like it's dying out.'

But the sense of approval—and Mrs Collins's smile—faded as quickly as it had appeared.

Of course she would have known all about the surrogacy agreement her daughter had arranged. She had probably been thrilled at the prospect of becoming a grandmother. Ellie felt a wash of sympathy and, in its wake, a renewed urge to see her closest friend. To get past the barrier that broken dreams had created.

If anybody knew where Ava was right now, surely it was—as Sue had suggested it would be—her mother.

'Mrs Collins?' Ellie stepped closer. Mr Jenkins had gone behind the counter and Luke was pulling some cash out of his pocket to pay for their sweets. She lowered her voice, anyway. 'I really need to get hold of Ava,' she said. 'Do you know where she is at the moment?'

Jill Collins shook her head sharply. 'I have no idea,' she muttered.

But her gaze slid away from Ellie.

She knew. She just didn't want Ellie to know.

Because she thought she might end up being responsible for a baby who was in no way related to herself?

Or was it because Ava had told her she wanted nothing more to do with Ellie?

Either way, it seemed that there was little Ellie could do. Except wait until fleeting eye contact was restored.

'If you talk to her,' Ellie said quietly, blinking back sudden moisture in her eyes, 'please tell her how much I'd like to hear from her. How much I'm missing my best friend.'

Luke had finished paying for their purchase but Ellie didn't feel remotely like tasting one of the chewy, chocolate covered little rectangles in her bag. Being brushed off by a woman who'd been like a second mother to her in her childhood hurt far more than she could have anticipated. It felt as if she wasn't wanted here.

To make matters worse, they arrived back at the house to find Mike the real estate agent pacing the veranda.

'Thank goodness,' he said, as soon as he saw them. 'I've got an offer written up here that's so hot it's burning my hands. You're not going to believe this...'

Ellie's heart sank to a new, low level.

Was this it?

The beginning of the end?

But Luke didn't follow Mike into the house, having opened the front door. He had turned to stare down the garden path towards the road.

'Who's that? Anyone you know, Ellie?'

She turned to see the male figure approaching and, this time, her heart dropped so hard and fast, she could feel it breaking.

'It's…it's Marco,' she whispered through dry lips that barely moved.

'Hey, Ellie.' Marco glanced at Luke but then ignored him as he moved closer. His smile was horribly reminiscent of the last one she'd seen on his face—just before his shocking attempt to kiss her—as if nothing could dent his confidence that he was about to get exactly what he wanted.

'It's about time I collected my son, don't you think?'

CHAPTER ELEVEN

LUKE STILL HAD one hand holding open the front door that was inclined to swing shut on its own. He still had his head turned, having heard the crunch of heavy footsteps on the shell path, so his body was twisted into a slightly awkward position but, for the life of him, he couldn't move.

It had been enough of a shock to find Mike on the veranda a minute ago and to realise he was about to face the final decision about walking away from the house and garden that were his last links to the people who'd made him the man he was today. He hadn't expected an outcome like this from the viewing. The house wasn't even officially on the market yet.

And this aftershock had been even less expected. Ellie had been confident that the man who'd fathered Jamie would not be returning. After she'd told him that Marco hadn't even wanted a baby in the first place, Luke had never given him another thought.

The shock was visceral. He didn't need to see the way the blood had drained from Ellie's face to know that life had just blindsided her yet again and her world felt as if it were crumbling around her.

Did he actually think he could swan in here and take Jamie?

His reaction was instant. And icy. *Over my dead body...*

'How did you...?' Ellie's voice was barely more than a whisper. Then she gave her head a tiny, disbelieving shake. 'Why are you here, Marco?'

'I told you. I've come for my son.'

'You didn't even want a baby. Ava told me.'

Marco's shrug was dismissive. 'A lot of things get said in the heat of a disagreement. I didn't mean it.'

But he hadn't even looked properly at Jamie, Luke noted. He was staring at Ellie, his gaze travelling up and down her body in a way that gave him a very unpleasant frisson.

Jealousy?

No. It was more the need to protect a woman from someone whose shallow intentions were all too clear.

'As for how I found you...' The hand gesture suggested it had been no problem. 'Once I discovered that your apartment had been burned to the ground, it was obvious where I needed to go for information about a missing person. Two missing people... The police were remarkably helpful when I explained that one of those missing people was my own son.'

Ellie took a step backwards. 'He's not your son, Marco. He's mine.'

Luke wanted to leap in and defend Ellie but he was still frozen, his brain throwing all sorts of unexpected things at him.

He'd never known his own father. Maybe that unknown man had never been aware that he'd become a father. Or had he tried to claim him and been sent away?

Would his own life have been very different if his father had had some part in it?

Okay, that history was totally different because Ellie hadn't abandoned Jamie. She adored him. He could hear her whisper in the back of his mind as clearly as if she'd just spoken again.

'I'd die for him,' she'd said that night. *'If it came to that.'*

The same night she'd listened to the sad story of his early life and had made him feel as though the bond between Ellie and Jamie and himself was powerful enough to last a lifetime.

When he'd promised that he would take care of Jamie if anything *did* happen to her.

And something was happening right now. Something that felt dangerous.

But…a biological father had rights, didn't he?

Luke had to fight the urge to launch himself off the veranda and forcibly remove this threat from Ellie's life.

My God…the way he was *looking* at her.

As if…

A truly horrible thought occurred to Luke then.

Had this baby been conceived naturally? It had been a private arrangement between friends, hadn't it? Maybe they hadn't even bothered using the services of a fertility clinic and an impersonal insemination.

But why did the notion seem unbearably painful?

He didn't have any claim on Ellie—past, present or future. He'd been the one to put the rules so firmly into place and Ellie hadn't seemed to mind that they could only ever be friends so maybe that was all she wanted as well—a few benefits because they were both consenting adults and happened to find each other more than a little attractive.

They were his rules. He'd lived with them for his entire adult life without them ever becoming such a problem.

Without them feeling so very wrong.

The pain morphed into anger. Anger at Mike, who was waiting inside the house for him to sign away one of the most precious things he'd ever had. At this stranger for turning up and making Ellie frightened. At himself for allowing something to happen that made him question the foundations of his life that had worked so well up until now.

And maybe he was even angry at Ellie, for being the common factor making all of these things suddenly become problems. For the sensation that he'd walked so far past any safe barriers that he was toppling over the edge of an unforeseen cliff.

He cleared his throat, which made both Ellie and Marco look in his direction.

'I think you'd all better come inside,' he snapped.

Mike looked surprised to see an extra person entering the house but he wasn't going to let it interfere with him doing his job.

'I don't mind waiting,' he assured Luke. 'I'll have a bit of a wander and admire the gardens again. I love what you guys have done out there in the vegetable patch. Could almost get inspired myself...'

'I'll have a coffee if there's one going,' Marco drawled. 'Unless you've got a cold beer in the fridge, mate.' He nodded in satisfaction when he stopped letting his gaze roam everywhere around the kitchen to stare through the French doors to the courtyard. 'Looks like the perfect spot to have a little chat out there.'

Luke looked as grim as Ellie had ever seen him. Furious, even.

Maybe he was fed up with having to rescue her from the disasters that her life seemed to be attracting? He had, after all, saved her life the day Jamie was born and then come to the rescue all over again on the night of the fire.

Or was it because he thought she'd lied to him when she'd said that Marco wasn't a problem? That she never expected to see him again and that it wouldn't matter if he did come back because she would never let him take Jamie away from her?

How naïve had she been?

He was her son's biological father. Of course he had rights in the eyes of the law.

And, if he genuinely wanted to be part of his child's life, Ellie would be perfectly happy to make that happen.

Well, perfectly happy was a stretch, but she would have been open to the prospect, but she just knew that Marco wasn't interested in Jamie. He hadn't even looked at him. Even now, when Jamie had woken to discover that he was hungry and wet and make his presence very obvious with his cries.

No. There was another reason that Marco had come here and Ellie felt a chill run down her spine as she realised that this vulnerable, precious baby she was holding was a means to an end as far as Marco was concerned.

Did he want to win Ava back, perhaps?

That might explain Jill Collins's oddly nervous reaction to meeting Ellie in Mr Jenkins' store. Had Marco also been trying to find Ava? Had she been worried about being able to protect her daughter from a man who'd already caused so much harm and would undoubtedly continue to do so if he got another chance?

Ava had been so much in love with Marco and Ellie knew there would be a danger that she could forgive him and try again—especially if there was the lure of a ready-made family. It was all too easy to allow fantasies to encroach on reality—look at the dreams she'd allowed herself to have of being the perfect family with Luke and Jamie?

Oh... God...

Would Marco fight to get full custody of Jamie? If he could persuade Ava to take him back, they'd present an option of a full family that the courts might decide was a better option than a single mother who had to work full-time and would still be struggling financially.

The thought was terrifying. The need to escape was fortunately easy to act on—at least temporarily—by excusing herself to change and feed Jamie. There was no way she was going to do that in front of Marco. He wouldn't look disconcerted at catching a glimpse of her breasts, the way Luke had that first time. He would probably revel in it.

Panic nipped at her heels as she dealt with Jamie's nappy. It wasn't until she had settled against the pillows of her bed and the hungry cries had been replaced with the contented sounds of sucking that she was able to let go of some of the horrible tension in her own body.

She stroked Jamie's cheek with a gentle finger and felt her determination take root and grow.

There was no way she would let Marco take Jamie

away from her. She would fight with everything she could muster.

Luke would help.

Or would he?

Maybe he was looking so furious because he had to wait to go through that offer on his property with Mike. Was he impatient to sign away any links with his past so he could move straight onto his exciting—unencumbered—future?

It suddenly became harder to hold onto the shreds of confidence that she could win the new battle that had appeared in her life. She didn't want to face this without the support that Luke could provide.

He hadn't even left the country yet but, already, she was feeling more alone than she ever had before.

Alone...and frightened.

The fear became strong enough to make her gasp a moment later, when Marco stepped into her room.

She didn't want to disturb Jamie or give him a fright by moving suddenly. She could only try and protect herself from the appreciative leer she was receiving by tugging her shirt to cover more of her breast.

'Just thought I'd pop in and see if you're ready to start talking,' he said.

'You need to leave,' Ellie told him. 'If you want any access to Jamie, you're going to have to go through the courts.'

'Ah... Ellie...' Marco lifted his hands. 'Don't be like that. We used to be so close. You and Ava and me... We were such good friends.'

'Ava was my friend,' Ellie said. 'I never liked you that much, to be honest, Marco. Maybe I knew you couldn't be trusted.'

'Maybe I couldn't be trusted because I was with the wrong woman.' Marco stepped closer to her bed and that was too much for Ellie. Jamie had to be close to the end of his feed now but even if he wasn't, she couldn't sit here feeling so exposed and vulnerable.

She wanted to call for Luke. Where was he?

Marco saw the way her gaze slid towards the door.

'I told him I was going to the loo.' Marco smiled. 'He's finding us a beer. Nice chap...'

Ellie was on her feet now. Putting Jamie on her shoulder, she tried to adjust her clothing before Marco could see anything more but the way he ran his tongue over his lips suggested that he'd already seen enough.

'We could make this work, Ellie,' he said. 'I've always fancied you—you know that. And now we've got a kid together...'

'Get out,' Ellie snapped as fear morphed into anger. 'Leave us alone.' She pushed past Marco as he reached out to touch her. She could hear his chuckle as she raced back towards the kitchen.

He'd never seen Ellie look like this before.

But Luke couldn't ask what had just happened to make her look so angry because he had Mike standing right beside him, reaching for one of the bottles of beer he had put on the outside table.

'Don't mind if I do.' Mike grinned. 'Although you might want to find some champagne soon, mate. You're going to want to celebrate, believe me.'

Mate?

He wasn't Mike's mate.

And he most certainly wasn't Marco's mate. He scowled at the man sauntering in Ellie's wake. The sooner he was gone, the better, but he needed to find out just how much of a threat he posed to Ellie. And it wouldn't do any of them any good to antagonise him.

Yet.

'Nice house,' Marco said. 'Not sure where you fit into the picture here, mate, but I'm sure Ellie will fill me in. Won't you, sweetheart?'

Luke's gaze clashed with Ellie's.

Sweetheart?

'Hey...' Marco seemed oblivious to the tension around him. 'Maybe I could stay for a while? You know...to get to know my son?'

'No.'

Luke and Mike and Ellie all spoke at precisely the same time. There was a moment's surprised silence then. Marco just grinned and shrugged. Then he stepped forwards and helped himself to a beer.

Ellie sank down on the bench seat at the far end of the table. Jamie seemed to be asleep but she clearly didn't want to put him into his bassinet or pushchair.

Mike seemed to feel obliged to fill the awkward silence. Or maybe he just couldn't wait any longer.

'You've got to have a look at this offer, Luke. The buyers are heading to Europe in a few hours and they want this signed and sealed before they take off, which is why they've put their best offer on the table. And it's a doozy... I've never seen anything like it.'

'You're selling up?' Marco took a swig of his beer. 'Hey, maybe I'd be interested. Looks like a great place to raise a kid and—bonus—the mother of my child is already living here.'

'It's not for sale,' Luke snapped. He caught the look of horror on Mike's face. 'Yet,' he amended. And it never would be to this person, he added silently—even if he could afford it. The thought of Marco being here, with Ellie and Jamie, was…well, it was disgusting, that was what it was.

An image came to mind of bringing Ellie here that night. Of her standing in his kitchen, the overlong arms of his jumper dangling as she hugged herself.

And another one, of how they'd made that first bed for Jamie in the old drawer.

They came thick and fast after that, as if a cork had been pulled from a bottle. Images that came with embedded emotions. Sensations, even…

That night that Jamie had been born and he'd sat on the end of her bed and realised how courageous Ellie was. That chin tilt that was so revealing about her determination to face a future when she had nothing more than her own courage to rely on. He'd seen it again, the night of the fire, when she'd been knocked back to square one all over again.

It didn't matter how big whatever she was facing was. Now he could see her pulling that very first weed out from between the paving stones of this courtyard, her eyes shining with the prospect of taking on the impossibly big task of taming this whole garden.

The way that white tee shirt with the bird and the hearts had been streaked with dirt. Nothing on how grubby she'd become out in the vegetable garden that day, mind you…and how incredibly delicious and sexy had that made her look?

Luke reached for a beer himself, to try and distract himself from this flood of memories but it didn't help. The taste of the beer only brought flashbacks of the pleasure it had given him, coming home to the food Ellie had so generously prepared so often.

That joke about how silly it was to ask whether he was hungry or not.

A joke that she'd used to let him know how much she wanted to go to bed with him but he'd seen through the bravado. He'd known how much she wanted it, but he'd also known how nervous she was.

Stop, he told his brain.

Just stop...

But how could it, when that memory rolled inexorably into the next? The sheer bliss of making love to this woman...

It hit him with such a jolt that he almost choked on his mouthful of beer.

He might have convinced himself that the kind of love he felt for Ellie Thomas was the kind that came with family or friendship but he'd been in denial, hadn't he?

He was in love with her. Totally and absolutely in love with her.

The one thing he'd never intended to happen—to have someone in his life that could potentially be left hurt or abandoned. And it wasn't just Ellie. There was Jamie as well. The baby with the most heart crunching smile ever. A baby he couldn't bear the thought of being another man's child.

Marco's child...

Luke tried to tune into the conversation that was going on between Mike and Marco but it was only a blur of sound.

It wasn't just Ellie or Jamie or Marco, Luke realised.

This was actually about himself. About the small

boy inside the man who had learned not to get attached to anything or anyone because it was inevitable that whatever was important in his life would get torn away from him.

The Gilmores had changed that because they were so determined.

He had learned to trust them.

But he'd learned to trust Ellie, too, hadn't he? Enough so that he had opened his heart to her and shared the sad story of his childhood and the fears he had of ever having a family of his own.

And hadn't he just reminded himself of how determined a person Ellie was?

Facing a future as a single mother.

Picking herself up after the disaster of the fire.

Tackling this huge garden bit by bit until she'd triumphed to the point of those rows of baby vegetable plants that she would never see turn into food that could grace platters on this old table.

Ellie wasn't joining in the conversation here, he noted. She was sitting silently, rubbing Jamie's back gently. Her head turned towards the pushchair nearby and Luke knew she was thinking of putting him down to sleep. Tucking him in with that cute little blanket with the ducks on it?

The blanket that had been one of the purchases on that crazy spending spree in the Baby Supermarket, where all those staff members had assumed that Luke was Ellie's partner and Jamie's father.

And, finally, Luke was swamped with the memory of how that had felt.

How *amazing* it had felt.

As if it would be the best thing that could happen to anyone. Ever.

Ellie's head was turning back towards the table now. Her gaze caught Luke's and locked onto it as securely as if a key had just been turned.

The connection was absolute.

Luke could feel her sadness and fear.

He could also feel her love. Not just for the tiny person she still held in her arms.

For *him*...

He could fight for this. To keep all of this. Okay, maybe they couldn't wave a magic wand and have Jamie's biological father disappear from their lives but they could manage it.

Together.

If that was what Ellie wanted as much as Luke did. He couldn't run away from this because, if he did, he would be running away from life, wouldn't he? The most important part of life, anyway...

He tried to tell her that, silently, in that long, intense gaze and something must have been communicated because he could see the lines of tension in her face soften.

And then he noticed the silence around them.

Were Mike and Marco intruding on what felt like the most private moment of his life?

No. They had both turned towards the kitchen. Towards a woman who was standing there, framed by the open French doors.

'Hope you don't mind,' the woman said. 'But the front door was open. I let myself in.'

Marco's jaw had gone slack. He looked nothing like the cocky young man who'd walked into their lives such a short time ago. Luke had no idea who this woman was but he liked her already because she had made Marco look so much less than happy.

Ellie, on the other hand, was looking thrilled. She was on her feet and moving towards the newcomer. Amazement had become the kind of pleasure that made anything else irrelevant. The wobble in her voice revealed how much this meant to her.

'Ava...'

CHAPTER TWELVE

THE HUG WAS kind of one-sided so that Jamie didn't get squashed between them but that didn't seem to affect its fierceness.

'I've been so worried about you,' Ellie growled.

'I know. I'm sorry, El. Mum told me how upset you looked.'

'Is that where you've been all this time? At your mum's? I thought you were flying somewhere.'

'I was. I did. I went to my aunt's place in the far north of Australia. But Mum kept calling and she finally persuaded me to come home a few days ago. She said I'd be safe in Kauri Valley...' Ava pulled back from the hug, far enough to look down at the tiny head nestled against Ellie's shoulder. 'Oh...' she breathed. 'He's gorgeous...'

Ellie nodded, tears misting her eyes. 'He's the best thing that's ever happened to me, Ava. I love him so much...'

Blinking hard, Ellie glanced up.

Seeking Luke's gaze again?

Of course she was. The way he had been looking at her just before Ava's dramatic entrance to the scene. As if he'd suddenly realised just how much he loved her. As much as she loved him...

And it hadn't been her imagination running away with her this time. He was still looking as if he never wanted to take his eyes off her ever again.

Okay... Jamie wasn't the only most amazing thing that had ever happened to her. Luke—and what they had found together—was a close second. Not even second, really. For Ellie, at least, it felt as if the three of them were bound together so closely it was hard to tell where the love for one separated from the love for the other.

They were family.

And maybe Luke felt the same way but was it enough to make him change his mind about those rules that had guided his life virtually for ever?

Ava straightened from bestowing a soft kiss to the top of Jamie's head. She turned from Ellie now and her body stiffened as she glared at Marco.

'You're the last person I expected to find here,' she said coldly.

Marco's gaze shifted. He looked as if he suddenly didn't want to be there at all but Ellie and Ava were standing in front of the doors into the house. If he wanted to escape, he'd have to head for the garden and he obviously didn't know that there were paths leading back to the road. He looked trapped.

Mike was looking uncomfortable, too. He knew where those paths were and he was staring at the side of the house as if weighing up his options of whether he should stay or not. Ellie saw him glance at Luke. Of course he was going to stay. There was a deal to be done, wasn't there?

'But why wouldn't you be?' Ava continued. 'You've been obsessed with Ellie, haven't you? What happened? Did the girl you ran off with realise what a bastard you really are and dump you?'

'Aww, don't be like that, babe.' Marco was attempting a winning smile. 'I came back to put things right. I still love you.'

Ava snorted. Ellie moved closer so that her shoulder was pressed against her friend's. Ava had her total support in escaping from her marriage once and for all.

'We can still be the family you dreamed of having.' But Marco didn't sound so sure of himself.

And Ava's tone was scathing. 'Not in this lifetime. I never want to see you again. Stay away from me. And stay away from my best friend.' Her glance at Ellie was a little uncertain. 'If that's what she wants.'

'Of course it is,' Ellie said. 'But...'

'But?' Ava's eyes widened.

'But he's Jamie's father,' Luke put in. 'However despicable the man might be, he's got some rights.'

Ava actually laughed. 'Is that what he told you? That he fathered this baby?'

Marco was on his feet now. Mike's jaw looked as if it were about to hit the floor.

Luke was looking bewildered and no wonder—Ellie was just as confused.

'But he is. It was his sperm that the clinic used.'

Ava's mouth twisted into a wry smile. 'Yeah...that's what we let everybody believe but it's not the real story, is it, Marco?'

Marco wasn't looking anywhere now. He had his head bent and his eyes shut.

'Marco's got a little problem,' Ava said. 'Well, more than one, let's be honest, but the one that's relevant is that his sperm mobility is abysmal. His swimmers weren't up to the job, apparently, and the only way to have any real chance of you getting pregnant, Ellie, was to use sperm from an anonymous donor. We all kept the secret to stop Marco's pride getting dented any further but I can't believe he thinks he can keep it up. To try and use a lie for whatever sneaky plan he's got in mind.'

'Oh, man…' Mike made a disgusted sound. 'You're a piece of work, aren't you, mate?'

Ava shook her head. 'He's crazy, that's for sure. For heaven's sake, the only person here who's actually got a claim on little Jamie is you, Ellie.'

Luke was getting to his feet.

'No,' he said. 'That's not true.'

He walked towards Ellie and reached out to gather Jamie from her arms. The look he gave her asked her to trust him and she didn't hesitate because there was something else in his gaze.

A promise that everything was going to be okay?

'I have a claim, too,' he said quietly. 'I gave Ellie a promise that I'd always be here to protect him if anything happened to her.'

He turned his head and smiled at her and Ellie's heart melted completely in the sheer warmth of it. The *love*…

'And things do happen to you, don't they, Ellie? Big things like becoming a mother and having your house burn down and having stupid people think they can scare you by threatening to take your son away.' Luke paused to take in a slow breath. 'I think you need me around on a permanent basis, don't you?'

Ellie's heart felt as if it were about to burst. If this was a proposal, it was the craziest ever.

And the best...

'I do,' she whispered. 'I *do*...'

Ava was looking from Luke's face to Ellie's and back again.

'That sounded like a wedding vow.' She grinned.

'It will be,' Luke murmured. 'I hope.'

Ellie couldn't say anything. She was drowning in love, here, unable to tear her gaze from Luke's. But she could nod. And she could move closer so that Luke could put his arm around her and hold her up because her knees had gone distinctly shaky.

Mike cleared his throat. He sounded more tentative than he ever had. 'That doesn't mean that you're going to take the property off the market, does it?'

'If that's what Ellie wants,' Luke said.

Ellie couldn't stop tears gathering at the enormity of what Luke was offering. His love would have been more than enough. This house and garden would be an astonishing bonus but it was more than that.

He was offering to share his past with her.

And his present.

And his future. Their future.

'It's exactly what I want,' she whispered. 'It's home... I think it was the moment I walked in here.'

Luke glanced at Mike. 'Well, that's that. Sorry. The house is definitely off the market.'

Mike's nod was resigned. 'Should have seen that coming, I guess. You two belong together. And you belong here.' He glared at Marco. 'You don't belong here, mate. Come on—I'll show you the way out.'

Ava watched them leave and then she took a deep breath and smiled at Ellie. 'We've got a lot to catch up on, haven't we?'

'We do.'

'Another time, maybe. I've never crashed someone's proposal before and I'm suddenly feeling like I'm more than a bit in the way.'

But Luke was smiling, too. 'Please stay,' he said. 'I'll put Jamie to bed and then I'll find a bottle of wine for you girls so you can catch up properly.' He bent his head to place a tender kiss on Ellie's lips. 'We've got the rest of our lives together.'

Ava's breath came out in a sigh as soon as they were alone.

'Wow...'

'I know...'

'That's *Luke Gilmore.*'

'I know.' Ellie could feel her smile stretching to rival one of Jamie's best efforts. He wasn't Kauri Valley High School's bad boy Luke Gilmore any more.

He was *hers*... Her best friend. Her lover. Her soul mate...

And the real miracle was that he felt the same way and the power of that love had been enough to make him realise that his rules had created a prison.

He was free.

Free to be with anyone he chose.

And he had chosen her...

'Sit down,' Ava ordered. 'And start talking. Unless you would rather I made myself scarce? I won't be offended or anything.'

But Ellie was smiling because she could still hear
Luke's last words—the most beautiful words she had
ever heard.

We've got the rest of our lives together.

* * * *

*If you enjoyed this story, check out these
other great reads from Alison Roberts*

*A LIFE-SAVING REUNION
THEIR FIRST FAMILY CHRISTMAS
THE FORBIDDEN PRINCE
THE FLING THAT CHANGED EVERYTHING*

All available now!

MILLS & BOON®
Hardback – July 2017

ROMANCE

MILLS & BOON®
Large Print – July 2017

ROMANCE

Secrets of a Billionaire's Mistress	Sharon Kendrick
Claimed for the De Carrillo Twins	Abby Green
The Innocent's Secret Baby	Carol Marinelli
The Temporary Mrs Marchetti	Melanie Milburne
A Debt Paid in the Marriage Bed	Jennifer Hayward
The Sicilian's Defiant Virgin	Susan Stephens
Pursued by the Desert Prince	Dani Collins
Return of Her Italian Duke	Rebecca Winters
The Millionaire's Royal Rescue	Jennifer Faye
Proposal for the Wedding Planner	Sophie Pembroke
A Bride for the Brooding Boss	Bella Bucannon

HISTORICAL

Surrender to the Marquess	Louise Allen
Heiress on the Run	Laura Martin
Convenient Proposal to the Lady	Julia Justiss
Waltzing with the Earl	Catherine Tinley
At the Warrior's Mercy	Denise Lynn

MEDICAL

Falling for Her Wounded Hero	Marion Lennox
The Surgeon's Baby Surprise	Charlotte Hawkes
Santiago's Convenient Fiancée	Annie O'Neil
Alejandro's Sexy Secret	Amy Ruttan
The Doctor's Diamond Proposal	Annie Claydon
Weekend with the Best Man	Leah Martyn

MILLS & BOON®
Hardback – August 2017

ROMANCE

MILLS & BOON®
Large Print – August 2017

ROMANCE

The Italian's One-Night Baby	Lynne Graham
The Desert King's Captive Bride	Annie West
Once a Moretti Wife	Michelle Smart
The Boss's Nine-Month Negotiation	Maya Blake
The Secret Heir of Alazar	Kate Hewitt
Crowned for the Drakon Legacy	Tara Pammi
His Mistress with Two Secrets	Dani Collins
Stranded with the Secret Billionaire	Marion Lennox
Reunited by a Baby Bombshell	Barbara Hannay
The Spanish Tycoon's Takeover	Michelle Douglas
Miss Prim and the Maverick Millionaire	Nina Singh

HISTORICAL

Claiming His Desert Princess	Marguerite Kaye
Bound by Their Secret Passion	Diane Gaston
The Wallflower Duchess	Liz Tyner
Captive of the Viking	Juliet Landon
The Spaniard's Innocent Maiden	Greta Gilbert

MEDICAL

Their Meant-to-Be Baby	Caroline Anderson
A Mummy for His Baby	Molly Evans
Rafael's One Night Bombshell	Tina Beckett
Dante's Shock Proposal	Amalie Berlin
A Forever Family for the Army Doc	Meredith Webber
The Nurse and the Single Dad	Dianne Drake

MILLS & BOON®

Why shop at millsandboon.co.uk?

Each year, thousands of romance readers find their perfect read at millsandboon.co.uk. That's because we're passionate about bringing you the very best romantic fiction. Here are some of the advantages of shopping at www.millsandboon.co.uk:

* **Get new books first**—you'll be able to buy your favourite books one month before they hit the shops

* **Get exclusive discounts**—you'll also be able to buy our specially created monthly collections, with up to 50% off the RRP

* **Find your favourite authors**—latest news, interviews and new releases for all your favourite authors and series on our website, plus ideas for what to try next

* **Join in**—once you've bought your favourite books, don't forget to register with us to rate, review and join in the discussions

Visit **www.millsandboon.co.uk**
for all this and more today!